THE BILLIONAIRE AND THE LIBRARIAN

ONCE UPON A BILLIONAIRE ROM-COM SERIES
BOOK 1

S.E. ROSE

Plot Assistance by The Fairy Plotmother
Editing by Judy's Proofreading

Couple Illustration © Celia Moscote
Cover Design by S.E. Rose

To Becca, who stayed up way too late, way too many nights in a row helping me plot this story. You made this pantser enjoy the plotting process.

CHAPTER ONE

Isa

Once upon a time, there was an asshole, and his name was Adam Wellington.

I stare at the unanswered email for the tenth time since I sat down at my computer. At least someone from his corporation wrote back when I reached out originally. But it was a form response asking me to submit my request in writing. As in, send it via snail mail.

I sigh as I stare at my screen as if willing his reply will make a reply appear. After a full minute, I slouch in my chair and promptly fall back on the floor as the entire chair flips over.

"Ouch," I manage as I stare up at the ceiling, questioning every choice I've ever made.

"Isa? Are you alright?" Ainsley asks from down the hall.

I roll out of the chair and rub the back of my head. "Yeah," I mutter.

I see her head pop around a shelf. "Sure?"

I grab the chair that's about as defunct as half the furniture in this library and set it back upright. "Yes. Just injured my pride again," I state as I give her a small smile.

"We should go down to the consignment shop and see if they have any new chairs. That chair is officially a death trap," she declares.

I don't have the heart to tell her that we don't even have the funds for a secondhand chair. "That's probably a good idea," I offer as I look around. It's nearly closing time. Ainsley walks over to the counter and starts to shut down the computer. She's been a great volunteer. When she walked in as a junior in high school and offered to work for free, I was suspect, but I don't know where I'd be without her. She's home from college for winter break and still offers to come help.

I glance out at the street. It's gotten dark, darker than normal for this time of day. I check my phone for weather alerts but don't see any. I know we're due for a little snow, but that's normal for this time of year. Still, my protective instincts don't like Ainsley driving in any snow at all.

"Ains, you should get going," I state. "I'll close up for the night."

She waves a hand at me. "I'm almost done. Plus, my weather app says we are only getting a dusting. No big deal."

I nod as she walks over and drops a pile of mail on my desk. "Any word on that grant you applied for?" she asks.

I shake my head. I had told her about the grant I had applied to weeks ago and offered up a possible special collection as a match. There was just one teeny-tiny problem. I hadn't gotten the special collection yet.

"What about that special collection? Has that asshat responded?" she inquires as she peers at me from over the top of the computer screen at the checkout desk.

"Not yet," I reply as I sort through the mail, trying not to grimace when I see two overdue bills.

"Well, I'm sure you'll hear back soon," she says as she grabs her coat and bag. "See you next Thursday."

"Oh right, have fun visiting your grandparents," I offer as she comes over and hugs me.

"Right. They have one television with basic cable. I just checked out like six books so I'm not bored," she says with a laugh.

"You guys are heading over there tonight?" I ask.

She nods. "My dad wants to get on the road soon, so we can bring them dinner and beat the snow."

"I'm sure they will love having you," I assure her.

She shrugs. "Later, Isa."

She waves as she walks out the door. I toss the bills down in a pile on my desk and shut down my computer. Looking across the room, I stare at the mural of Storyview Falls. The legend is that the name of the town came from waterfalls hidden in the forest that had magical powers. But modern historians believe the waterfalls weren't magical, and instead of being inland, they are out by the cliffs near the beach. Either way, it made for fun wall art for the library.

I grab my gym bag and purse and head out the door, making sure it locks behind me. I walk next door to the little bakery below my apartment. The door chimes as I walk inside.

"We're closed," Elisha's voice rings out from the back.

"Well, thank God for that. I hear this place sucks," I answer as I drop my bags.

Elisha comes out of the kitchen and glares at me. "Well, fuck you very much, ho."

"You're fucking welcome, slut. Also, maybe try locking your door when you close, otherwise, any riffraff can just walk right in," I reply with a wink.

She laughs as she throws a dish towel over her shoulder. She walks over to the counter and grabs a bag. Handing it to me, she motions to the few chairs in the little bar area of the bakery. I sit down and she reaches into the bag and places a muffin in front of me. Elisha has been feeding me since the second day I moved in above her café. She told me that I looked like I needed a dozen donuts and promptly set a box of them in front of me after I asked for a small coffee because that's all I could afford. I tried to pay her, and she refused. Later she told me she would never accept money from a woman whose purse was literally sewn back together in three places. I told her that was prejudiced against consignment shoppers, and she pulled out her used handbag. After that, we became best friends. She's like the older sister that I never had, and I don't know what I'd do without her...and also her stellar baking skills.

"Eat and tell me what's going on?" she demands.

"Geez, pushy much?"

She shrugs. "You love it."

Laughing, I unwrap the muffin as she reaches over and pulls out two bottles of water, placing one in front of me.

I take a bite of the carrot cake muffin and groan. "You are a freaking culinary genius," I mumble as I swallow my first bite.

"I know," she agrees.

"Wow, humble much?"

"You know it. Stop stalling, did that asshole reply to your emails yet?" she asks, giving me a pointed look.

Sighing, I take another bite and shake my head because I'm pretty sure if I speak, I'll burst into tears. When I heard about this first-edition collection, I knew it was my only chance to show this charity that I had a match of some kind to contribute toward the grant award, because I certainly didn't have any money or personnel.

Elisha sits up and curses under her breath. "Fuck this. Just drive up to that crusty old jerk's estate and refuse to leave until he sees you!"

I choke on the muffin and reach for the water as Elisha pats my back. Once I've composed myself, I stare back at her. "You can't be serious."

"Do I look like I'm kidding?"

"Well, no, but...I can't just drive out there," I say, my voice dropping to a whisper.

"Yes. You can. It's literally less than ten miles away," she assures me.

"Fuck. You can't be serious. What would I even say?" I ask in semi-horror.

Elisha reaches out and grips my shoulder. "You look that over-entitled prick in the eyes and say, loan me your damn fantasy-book collection."

"They are Jane Austen and James Joyce first editions," I correct her for the millionth time. Elisha is a fantasy-book lover and refuses to accept that other genres exist.

"Fine, whatever. Just go ask him. Also, you should ask if he has any first-edition fantasy novels. What's the worst thing that can happen?" she prods.

"He has me arrested for trespassing and I end up in a cell with a bunch of drunk people who vomit all over me and my parents can't get there to bail me out and I have to spend the weekend in vomit-covered clothing locked up with a metal toilet and no toilet paper," I state.

"Ewww. No. Just no. That's not happening," she says, her eyes wide at the faux horror I just envisioned.

"OK, well, it could be close to that."

Elisha drops her hand and stares into my eyes. "Isabelle Lisette Garren, you need to put on your lady balls and do it!"

I hate that she's right. I hate that I need to do this. "OK," I state because clearly, I've lost my ever-loving mind.

Her dark eyes widen. "OK, like you're going to do it?"

I nod. "Yeah, why not. I hate to admit it but you're right. My time is up. I just got the final notice on the library's electric bill."

"I can't believe the city council is making the library pay their electric bill. It's so messed up," Elisha says as she starts grabbing various pastries, muffins, and cookies and stuffing them into two bags which she pushes toward me. "Here. Take these. No one can say no to my pastries or cookies. Not even stingy old men."

"I don't think he's that old. Or at least the photo on the company website doesn't look like he's that old."

"Whatever. He's a douche," she grumbles.

Shrugging, I finish my muffin and grab the bag of food that I know will have to sustain me through the weekend, although I'd never admit that to Elisha, but I'm pretty sure she knows based on how many muffins and bagels she shoved into one of the bags.

"Go get 'em, lady!" Elisha cheers me on as I walk to the door. "Give him hell!"

"That's right, Adam Wellington! You're about to meet your match," I mutter to myself as I get into my car that's parked along Main Street. It takes three attempts to start it, but when it purrs to life, I breathe a sigh of relief and drive down the street to pick up my dog on the way to Wellington Estate. What's the worst thing that can happen? He says no and I go back home. Yep, that would be the worst thing for sure. Aside from that whole trespassing, arrest, and jail-with-a-metal-toilet thing.

CHAPTER TWO

Isa

"Come on, you just peed like five seconds ago," I groan as I pull my dog, Felipe, toward my car.

He wags his tail happily and starts to dig up the dirt. "Fuck, come on, you literally just got bathed," I scold as I wave to my mom's friend Mrs. Huber who graciously washes Felipe once a month for a fraction of the price. In return, I waive her late fees at the library. Quid pro quo.

Felipe sees a cat down the road and nearly launches me into oncoming traffic. There's a reason I don't attempt to clean my Great Dane on my own, he weighs more than me, and my bathroom would not survive it.

"Are you trying to kill me?" I ask him as I pull on his lead and he magically sits down and gives me a giant dog grin with his tongue hanging out.

"You know, when you do that, it's very hard to stay mad at you?"

He barks his agreement and I roll my eyes as I open my car door and usher him inside.

"We have one stop on the way home, buddy," I say as I pull out onto Main Street, heading out of town. The clouds are thickening in the sky, and I shiver as I look up at them. A dusting my ass, there's at least two inches of snow up there.

I contemplate turning around but it's only five more miles to the turnoff for the Wellington Estate. No one comes out here. Ever since Christopher and Janet Wellington were killed in a car crash, it's almost like the estate is empty, but I know Adam Wellington is out here. People see him on rare occasions, but mostly it's because of his personal chef, Bastian Greer, who is dating the chef who owns our local pub. Bastian is a hoot and I have a feeling he's the exact opposite of Adam Wellington if I was a betting woman, which I'm not.

My cell phone rings, and I press the speaker button and answer it. "Hi, Dad," I state as I turn on my windshield wipers, which only smear the snow instead of wiping it away.

"Hey, turtle dove, I just wanted to make sure you got home, it looks like we're getting more than a dusting."

"Yeah, I can see that, I just have to make a quick stop and then I'll be home."

"Good, good. How's that grant situation, kiddo?"

"It's...uh, going..." I stammer. Ugh. I may have decided to do all this grant stuff on my own. I know my parents would help me out, but I want to accomplish it without them. I just want to make them proud, and I'm not ready to give in yet.

"Well, give that Adam kid hell. I hear he's nothing like his old man," Dad encourages.

"I will. I should go, Dad. I'll talk to you later," I say as I disconnect right before turning off on Wellington Lane, home to one house...if you can call it that...the thing is a monstrosity.

The house emerges as I drive up a lane that's covered by

trees. Even in the dead of winter, the branches form a thick tunnel that keeps the view of the estate hidden until you reach the end of it. And then it's there, Wellington Estate. I've not ever been out here, just catching glimpses of it through a nearby apple orchard. It looks sort of like a castle with turrets and stones and a big wooden front door.

"All this place needs is a moat with alligators," I say to Felipe as he too leans forward to take in the colossal dwelling.

"Here goes nothing," I state as I park my car and open the door. Felipe jumps out and I glare at him.

"Buddy, I don't think you're welcome inside," I say as I reach into the passenger side and grab the pastries that Elisha gave me as a peace offering.

The front door opens, and I look up to see Bastian struggling with a backpack that even on his tall frame looks enormous. He pauses mid shoulder-strap adjustment and looks at Felipe and then me.

"Uh...hey, Isa...and Felipe," he manages as his eyes widen. Everyone in town knows my dog, mostly because we look ridiculous every time we walk down Main Street. I probably should just ride him like a small horse instead of pretending I am some sort of dog owner who can control my canine that could easily drag me in any direction.

"Hey," I reply as I yank on Felipe's leash, and he sits and tilts his enormous head to the side. I don't have to look at him to know his tongue is hanging out and he's waiting for Bastian to come pet him and also give him a treat because that's their normal interaction. Why Bastian always has dog treats in his pockets is a question that's been on the tip of my tongue many times, but I've always been too shy to ask, and to be fair, half the time, I'm in the middle of listening to a good audiobook and don't want to pause it to have a social interaction. Dog-walking time equals audiobook reading for me. And all the times we've hung out at Elisha's café, it's never once crossed my mind.

Bastian looks around as if the reason for my sudden appearance out here is going to fall out of the sky along with the snow. He quickly steps back inside and waves his hand for us to come into the house...house? Can you really call this thing a house?

I stop questioning my internal dialogue and quickly pull Felipe inside.

Bastian shuts the door as we stand in a giant three-story entryway. Shit. This is way, way nicer than I expected.

There's artwork on the walls that looks to be original. And when I say artwork, I mean famous paintings that people learn about in high school art classes. The crystal chandelier that hangs overhead probably cost more than my parents' home and half of Main Street.

I look down and see my shoes dripping onto the floor and I cringe.

"What brings you out here?" Bastian asks.

"Is Mr. Wellington home?" I ask.

Bastian swallows and nods. "He is," he answers slowly. Bastian seldom brings up his boss. All I know about Adam Wellington is he is rich, he doesn't hang out on Main Street, and Bastian cooks food for him and met him in France a long time ago.

Now, I'm the one swallowing my nerves. "I was hoping to see him. I've been trying to get in touch with him for a few months now and I just thought I'd stop by with some treats and see if he won't consider my request to borrow some books," I explain as I hold up the bag Elisha gave me. I haven't said anything to Bastian about the books because I feel bad dragging him into it. I may have mentioned it once, but Bastian just suggested I send an email, which I did, ten times.

"Elisha's?" he asks.

I open it and hold out a cookie which he accepts and takes a bite of. He groans in appreciation. "She is a freaking genius," he mumbles in between bites.

"Right?" I reply. I nervously adjust my weight from one foot to the other and back again. "So, is he here?"

Bastian nods as a door opens in the distance and I hear footsteps. I straighten and try to look presentable. I'm readying myself to speak to Adam Wellington when a short woman who appears to be slightly older than my parents appears from around a corner. She startles and places a hand on her chest.

"Oh my! You scared me!" she says as she tries to compose herself.

"Mrs. Potter, this is Isa Garren. She'd like to speak to Adam," Bastian explains.

"Oh?" Mrs. Potter frowns. "He's in his office on a call. But maybe he could speak to you when he gets off? It might be a little while though."

"I can wait..." I trail off as I look at Felipe. I can't exactly leave him in the car for a long time in this weather.

Mrs. Potter looks at Felipe. "Well, we can't have..." She pauses.

"Felipe," I state as I pat his head and he looks up at me with a goofy doggy grin.

"Felipe," she repeats, "waiting outside. Let's get you settled in the drawing room, and I'll let Mr. Wellington know you are here when he gets off his call."

"Thank you. I really appreciate that," I say.

"Of course," she says as she motions for me to follow her.

Bastian looks out of the windows surrounding the door.

"Uh, no offense, but don't stay too long. I'm not sure your car is equipped for the snow," he mumbles.

I roll my eyes. "Me and Bessie will be just fine," I assure him.

"Bessie?" he asks.

I shrug. "It's her one mismatched black door," I explain, as I glance out at my white car. After I got in an accident a few years ago, the repair guy could only find a black door. It was extra to paint it white, so I just kept it black and put some black spot stickers that look like cow prints on my car.

"Nice...cow stickers?" he stammers.

"Thanks. It completes her look," I reply with a wink.

He laughs and shakes his head. "How have I never seen your car before?"

"I keep her hidden just off Main Street." I look outside. "I think we are only getting a few inches," I add.

"That's what..." He trails off as Mrs. Potter raises an eyebrow.

He presses his lips together, but I can see him fighting a grin. "You know we have a winter storm warning now, right?"

I shake my head and frown in confusion. "No."

"Well, it just came through. So don't wait too long," he says.

I nod. "Thanks. I won't," I assure him.

"See you Monday, Mrs. Potter," Bastian adds with a wave as he opens the door to leave. A brisk wind blows in, and I shiver as he shuts it.

"Come along now. Can I get you some coffee or tea while you wait, dear?" Mrs. Potter asks as I begin following her down a long corridor into a room that seems quaint in comparison to the entryway, yet is still far more opulent than any room I've ever been inside.

"Oh, uh sure. Tea, please," I say as I sit at a small table in the corner of the room.

I hear yelling coming from somewhere and Mrs. Potter glances toward the door and then back at me. She gives me a sad smile. "He's...not in the best of spirits today. Just so you know."

Great, I think, just great. I nod as she leaves me to wait. Felipe lies down next to me with his head on his paws. I pull my phone out and realize I have like one bar. I try to open an app but I don't have enough service. Groaning, I chuck the phone back into my purse.

I've barely begun looking around the room when Mrs. Potter is back with tea. Like a full-on silver tray with cream and sugar and a pot of tea. I'm almost afraid to drink from the fine china which probably costs more than my car. She even brought a small bowl of water for Felipe and sets it down in front of him. He starts slurping it up immediately.

"Thank you," I whisper.

"Of course. Do you need anything else? I'm about to pop out to my cottage before the trail gets too slippery. But I've messaged Mr. Wellington. I'm sure he'll be here shortly."

"Oh, you live out here?" I ask.

She nods. "My husband, Thomas, and I live at the edge of the property in the caretaker's cottage. Makes for an easy two-mile walk every day," she explains.

My eyes widen. "Two miles?"

"Well, nearly two miles. Keeps us fit," she says with a smile. "Can I get you anything while you wait?"

I shake my head.

"The kitchen is just down the hallway, fifth door on the left if you need anything at all, help yourself, dear," she says.

"Thank you," I reply.

"Of course. It's my pleasure. It's just so nice to have someone visit," she adds as she nods and leaves me before I have a chance to ask when the last visitor was.

"Well, I guess it's just you and me, kid," I say as I look at Felipe. He pants and licks my hand.

I take a sip of tea and am about to look around when out

of nowhere, two giant rottweilers come barreling into the room. They start barking and Felipe starts barking and then all three of them take off, running out of the room into the corridor before I can grab Felipe's leash. Damn it!

I set down my teacup and begin running after them, down one corridor and then another, and suddenly Felipe presses his head into a wooden door, and it opens. I can hear a voice on the other side. Oh no! I hustle to the doorway where all three dogs are wrestling in the middle of what looks to be a very expensive rug in front of a very large mahogany desk. My eyes look to the man sitting behind it. He looks...ferocious? Is that possible? He's sporting a beard. His hair is a mess as if he's been yanking on it. And his very piercing blue eyes are gazing upon me as if I'm an intruder here to rob him.

"I'll have to call you back," he grunts as he disconnects a call on his desk phone.

"Who the hell are you?" he yells, "And what the hell is that?" he adds, motioning to Felipe.

FUCK! It's Adam Wellington. This is not the introduction I was hoping for.

CHAPTER THREE

Adam

"Ames! Isaac! Heel!" I yell. My dogs freeze and immediately take sitting positions in front of me. I'm already irritated. Fucking James Titan is going down. If he even thinks he can wage a hostile takeover of my company, he has another thing coming. I was about to deliver that message to him when a horse-sized dog came running into my office followed by my two rottweilers. They were immediately followed by a woman who I don't know.

I look back to the woman whose mouth is hanging open. She closes it and opens it again like a fish.

"Who are you?" I repeat.

My eyes are drawn to her slender neck as I watch her throat muscles contract as she swallows. Her eyes blink twice from behind black-rimmed glasses. She clears her throat and gives her head a little shake. "I'm Isabelle Garren. I've been trying to contact you about—"

I wave my hand. "Not interested," I growl. I feel the anger

pulsing through my veins. Why in the hell did my staff let her in here?

"Mr. Wellington, if you would just hear me out," she begins as she steps toward my desk. Her dog, or at least I suspect the dog is hers because it sure as fuck isn't mine, that has been rolling around on my floor, gets up and walks over to her. She pats his head and looks at me. "I'm the town librarian and I would like to borrow some of your first-edition books for a special exhibit."

You have got to be fucking kidding me. This woman is here for some damn books.

I can't help the sound that escapes my throat. It comes out as a low growl of disgust. "Get out," I say in a barely audible whisper from behind clenched teeth.

She shuffles her weight from one foot to the other but doesn't move. Then she crosses her arms and glares at me.

"No," she says. "Not until you agree to loan me your books."

"Get the hell out of here," I say more loudly than before.

"No," she repeats.

I slam my hand on my desk, and she gives a little jump but still doesn't move. I walk around my desk, and as I do, Ames and Isaac walk in front of her and sit. Their low growls startle me.

Her lips curl up into a smirk. Something about that awakens my cock. Nothing has awakened that beast in ages. Why is this mess of a woman affecting my body? I don't like it.

"I don't accept solicitors at my residence," I restate as I cross my arms, mirroring her stance. I glare down at her. She's tiny, barely over five feet tall. Her small stature has a memory creeping into the recesses of my brain. I quickly bat it away. I'm not going to let myself dwell on things that can't be.

"Well, it's a good thing that I'm not a solicitor. As I was saying, I'm the librarian at the—"

"Yeah, I got that. I don't care. Get out," I say, pointing to the door.

Her jaw clenches and she narrows her eyes. "If you would just give me the books, I will be happily on my way."

I laugh. "That's your pitch? Seriously?"

I see her chest rise and fall on a deep breath. "No, but you don't seem like someone who can be reasoned with."

"I can be reasoned with," I assure her.

She raises one dark eyebrow. "Really?"

"Yes. You just aren't very persuasive."

She rolls her eyes. "Well, you aren't a very good host."

"I didn't invite you into my home. You're trespassing," I state dryly.

She groans. "Is lending a few books really that big of a deal?" she asks as she looks around my office and motions to our surroundings with her hands. "I'm pretty sure that you won't miss them, and they'll be back here before you know it."

"Still no," I say as I step around her and my dogs, and motion for her to leave my office.

"We can provide signage indicating that the Wellington family has lent them to the library," she adds.

"Yeah, guess who's still not interested." I point to my chest and then back toward the hallway. I look out into the hall, wondering where my staff are. I pull out my phone and see two missed text messages.

Ms. Potter: Your evening meal is in the warmer in the kitchen, per your request. Mr. Potter and I are leaving for the evening. I've shown your visitor into the parlor. Please, call if you need me.

Bastian: (five laughing emojis) You have a visitor. (five laughing emojis)

That fucker. Bastian is lucky that I consider him a friend, or his ass would be fired.

I glance back over at Miss Holier-Than-Thou Librarian. What was her name? Isabelle?

Yes, Isabelle Garren.

I clear my throat. "Ms. Garren, I am not seeing visitors today. Please send your request to my staff and it will be addressed through the proper channels," I manage through gritted teeth. The audacity of this woman. If I wasn't in such a piss-poor mood, I'd almost be impressed by her stubbornness.

"Funny you should mention that. I have," she replies with a deadpan stare.

"Wonderful, then I'm sure they will be back in touch with you shortly," I say as I motion for what must be the tenth time, to the hallway.

She shifts her weight again and cocks her head to one side. "Are your staff inept?" she asks, raising that eyebrow at me again.

I feel my face begin to flush with anger. "No," I growl.

"Oh, because I have emailed. Then, as instructed, written my request. And then emailed again. Ten times to be exact over three months. Yet, I have received nothing more than a form response. So, please tell me how great your staff are," she says as her hand releases from her crossed arms to make a motion for me to continue.

I take a step back toward her and point at her chest. "My staff are the best. And if they haven't replied to your request, it is because the request is not of importance to my very large corporation. Now leave."

We both stand, chests heaving as we stare at each other. For a split second, I think she isn't going to budge, but then she closes her eyes for a brief moment. I look down at her long, dark lashes resting on her freckle-dotted cheeks. Even through her glasses, I can see she wears no makeup. Her beauty is one hundred percent natural. A single curly tendril of hair escapes her bun and falls across her cheek. For reasons that I can't explain, my hand itches to reach out and tuck it behind her ear. She beats me to it.

She licks her lips and I watch as her tongue dampens the pink skin. Her cheeks heat under my stare and she looks down at her dog, who has joined mine at her feet.

"Come on, Felipe. Let's go," she says quietly as she steps around me and walks out of my office. I follow her because unlike what she thinks, I'm not a monster and I'm certainly aware of how to be a good host, I just chose not to host, not anymore.

Her heels click on the marble tiles of my foyer floor as she walks across the grand entryway toward the doors. She turns the knob and nothing happens. I fight the urge to roll my eyes and call my staff to see her out because all of my staff have left for the evening.

So instead, I step behind, reaching for the handle myself. For the briefest of moments, our hands touch and an electric current passes between our fingers. Ms. Garren swiftly pulls her hand back. I take a breath, steadying myself from what I can only assume is static electricity, and I rattle the doorknob as I press outward. The door creaks open and a blast of snow blows in at us.

I feel her shiver with her back pressed against my front. I peer outside. It's a full-on blizzard. Were we expecting snow? I squint trying to see into the darkness beyond the light of my front door. All I see is white and a car. It's mostly coated in snow now, but I can make out enough to know that the car is not road-worthy on a sunny day, much less on one like today.

I pull the door closed and step back.

Ms. Garren's dog sits next to her staring up at me as

though I'm a god or a mythical creature that will give him treats on demand. I look from him to her. She's staring at me in total confusion.

"W-what are you doing?" she asks, her eyes wide with confusion and…fear? Is she afraid of me?

"You can't drive home in that," I state. Memories that I wish I didn't have, begin to unfurl from the crevices in my brain where I pushed them. I feel my jaw clench and all my muscles tighten. My answer is non-negotiable. No one and I mean no one will be driving in that weather. Not on my watch.

She rolls her eyes. "Of course, I can," she says as she spins back around and grabs the doorknob. I step around her, pushing her hand off my door.

"No. You can't. You may stay the night. You can drive home once the roads are cleared tomorrow," I announce.

"I have a car and I know how to drive in the snow," she grumbles and crosses her arms again as she turns around and faces me again.

I laugh sarcastically. "That," I say, motioning to the car that's beyond the door, "is not a car. That is a death trap."

I reach over her and bolt the door by turning the giant skeleton key. Then I remove it and slip it into my pocket.

I hear her sharp intake of breath as I lean over her. I pull back and look down at her.

"You're staying here. End of discussion," I snarl as I give her a pointed look before turning and walking away.

CHAPTER FOUR

Isa

Did I just get kidnapped? Is locking me in his mansion kidnapping? Well, either way, it's most definitely illegal. There is no way in hell that I'm spending the night in a stranger's home. This guy is a total jerk!

"Where do you think you're going?" I ask as I jog after him with Felipe, Ames, and Isaac in tow. I hadn't even realized that his dogs had followed me to the front hall.

He has the audacity to not respond. He just keeps walking back toward his office.

"Will you wait up for two seconds?" I ask as I try to keep up with him.

He pauses at the door. I wait for a response.

"Will you please just stay the night?" His voice trembles as if it's taking all his restraint not to yell at me.

"Why should I?" I ask, my hands going to my hips.

He turns and faces me. His eyes take in my stance, and I

swear I see the corner of his mouth twitch as if he's fighting a smile.

When his eyes reach mine, he searches them for a long beat before he speaks.

"If you stay…I'll consider your request," he says.

I feel my eyes involuntarily widen. "Are you serious?"

"Yes."

"I don't have to…" I trail off because I realize how ridiculous I sound. Of course, this man wouldn't want me like that. Look at him! Even with his beard and messy hair, he's still the epitome of sophistication. Mr. Wellington is dressed in a white button-down shirt that looks more expensive than any clothing I own. He's wearing black pants that fit him too perfectly because they were probably tailored just for him. And his shoes. His shoes look like they could be in an ad for expensive fine leather. And then there's the watch. Patek Philippe. I only know of that brand because I read an article about it. Most people wouldn't have a clue. Understated wealth emits from him like he's a projector in a movie theater.

His eyes narrow. "You don't have to what?"

I grimace at his stern voice. "Never mind…I…" I pause as I weigh his offer. Do I say yes? No? He's not wrong, driving home in that snowstorm would be an irresponsible thing to do. His house is big enough to have guest rooms and he clearly has dog food. He doesn't seem like a serial killer…well, not really. And Bastian is his friend and Bastian definitely wouldn't be friends with a serial killer, at least not knowingly. With a sigh, I nod. "I accept your offer."

"Good." He runs a hand through that messy hair. There's something oddly attractive about that motion. I chalk up my irrational thoughts to stress from being stuck in this mansion with the beastly man in front of me. "I'll show you to the east wing. You can sleep there," he states. He shuts his office door and starts back down the hall. I follow him, still with three dogs in tow.

"The kitchen is down that hallway," he says, pointing down a long and narrow corridor.

I nod my understanding. We go up the grand staircase. We make a left and then a right and then a left.

"Could have used a transporter? Will we be there by tomorrow?" I mutter under my breath.

He pauses and turns to look at me, a motion that now feels like a norm between us because he's done it at least a half dozen times this evening.

"What did you say?" he asks.

"Beam me up, Scottie?" I state as my explanation.

He shakes his head slightly and turns back around. We walk past three doors in silence. He pauses at the last one.

"This is the gym...in case you wanted to work out," he says as he opens the door to show me the inside of the room. It's a state-of-the-art gym, similar to the one in town. It has everything you would need including fresh fluffy, white towels, television sets, yes sets, as in plural, and a water and ice machine. I roll my eyes as if I'm going to work out tonight. But then, I remember that my gym bag is in my car. And that means, I have some toiletries and clothes.

"I...I have a bag in my car, a gym bag with some clothes," I say, mostly to myself.

I see his jaw tic. "I will go get it. Wait here," he says.

"I..." I trail off as he rushes past me and disappears around a corner. I turn to follow him, but he's already gone. Was it two rights and a left or a right, left, right? I try to remember the way back to the stairs. I'm gonna need a map or some breadcrumbs.

I'm just about to attempt to find him when Mr. Wellington appears around the corner. His hair and beard still have some snow on them and he's holding my bag.

"Here," he says, shoving it toward me. "By the way, try locking your car door from now on." Oops.

I take it. "Uh, thanks," I manage as he walks past me. We go around one more corner. The hallway ends with giant double doors. He opens them and turns on a light.

I begin to take in the room. It's enormous. Easily two stories high with a giant four-poster bed against the far wall. There's a bay window that faces the wall opposite us. Large oversized chairs sit facing each other in front of a fireplace.

I see two doors to my right. I'm about to ask where they lead when Felipe barrels past me and jumps onto the bed.

"Felipe!" I shriek, charging after him. "Get off the bed!"

I go to grab him, but Ames and Isaac join him on the bed and there's no way I'm going to wrangle all three of them off the bed.

"Heel," Mr. Wellington commands as he snaps his fingers.

The dogs look at me. I bite my lip to keep from laughing.

"Ames! Isaac! I said, heel!" he repeats.

The dogs whine but slowly get down and slink over to him with their tails tucked between their legs. They sit in front of him but keep giving me glances as if unsure which master they should be listening to.

"Are they...guard dogs?" I ask.

He nods.

I bite my lip again.

"What?"

"They just...aren't very scary. I would have thought you'd own some sort of dog like Cujo," I explain.

He gives me a deadpan stare.

I shrug.

"Mr. Wellington," I begin.

He holds up his hand. "Please...Adam...just Adam," he states.

I raise an eyebrow surprised by his insistence on informality. I guess I should try to be nice. The guy is attempting to keep me safe, and he's offered me this enormous guest suite.

"Right, Adam, thank you for..." I motion around us.

"Of course." He pauses as if contemplating saying something more, but instead turns toward the door. "There's a bathroom and closet off your room. You are free to go wherever you like except my office and the west wing." He glances back over his shoulder to make sure I understood him.

"The west wing?" I ask. I want to make some snide comments about the White House, but I refrain.

"Anything on the opposite side of the staircase," he explains.

I nod. "Fine. I'll stay on the starboard side," I tease because honestly, I'd probably get lost finding this off-limits west wing.

I see that faint twitch in his lips again. Does this man have some sort of issue with smiling?

"Goodnight," he adds. "Ames, Isaac."

The dogs don't budge and Adam sighs. "Fine, stay," he huffs as he closes the door.

The dogs give me one look and then go back to the bed where they join Felipe. Thank God it's some sort of California king because these three canines take up a lot of space.

I open one of the doors across from me. A walk-in closet. I see some things inside, but I'm too tired to explore. I open the other door and am greeted by an enormous bathroom. Marble as far as the eye can see. Fancy.

I grab my bag and make quick work of putting on one of several workout outfits I keep in it. It'll have to do. I grab my extra phone charger and go to plug in my phone. I still barely have a bar of service out here. I send off a message to Elisha.

Me: Snowed in with Mr. Warm and Friendly. Hopefully will be able to get home tomorrow.

Elisha: What? You're out at the Wellington Estate still?

Me: Yep. (deadpan emoji)

Elisha: I guess my cookies did more than they were supposed to. (winking emoji)

Me: What? Ewww. No way. He forbade me from driving in the storm.

Elisha: Forbade? OK, Jane Austen.

Me: (eye-rolling emoji)

Elisha: You better get the books!

Me: He said if I stayed, he'd give them to me.

Elisha: Interesting. Also, creepy.

Me: Don't worry. I just locked the door to this guest room.

Elisha: Remember *The Secret Garden* movie?

Me: (eye-rolling emoji) I'll be fine. I'm sure he won't sneak in here through a secret passage.

Elisha: Do you have Felipe with you?

Me: I do.

Elisha: Good. Stay safe.

Me: Will do.

I send my parents a text to let them know where I am and then put my phone down and curl up on the bed in between the dogs. This has got to be the strangest day I've had lately... maybe ever. Things could definitely not get weirder. That's for sure.

CHAPTER FIVE

Adam

Beep. Beep. Beep.

I groan as I roll over and tell my alarm to turn off. The room is quiet. Very quiet. And that's when I remember two things. One, my dogs are in the blue guest room on the far side of the house with my unexpected houseguest who holds some strange power over them. And two, it snowed last night. I wonder how much we ended up getting.

Instead of checking my weather app, I get out of bed and walk over to the blackout curtains covering my balcony doors. Flinging them open, I stare out into...a blizzard?

"What in the actual fuck?" I mutter.

I walk back over to my phone and pull up the weather app.

Warning.

Blizzard conditions for East Provincial County will continue through the day. Wind gusts over 50 miles per hour are expected. Snow accumulation is twenty-eight to thirty inches. Expect whiteout conditions through late afternoon.

Snow is expected to taper overnight with a light snow continuing tomorrow. An additional 2–4 inches is expected tomorrow.

I'm about to click on the interactive radar map when a text message pops up.

Cory: Your 9 a.m. is now virtual. Flights are suspended.

Guess I'm not taking the helicopter.

Another message pops up.

Mrs. Potter: Good morning, dear. Mr. Potter and I are snowed in out here. I packed some extra meals last night just in case. They are labeled and in the freezer. Hopefully, Ben will be able to get the paths plowed tomorrow. Let me know if you need anything and I'll do my best.

Me: Please stay put. I'll be fine.

I barely finish responding when another message pops up.

"For fuck's sake," I mumble. "It's Grand Fucking Central Station on this damn phone."

Bastian: Won't be at work today, boss.

Me: No fucking shit, Sherlock.

Bastian: What? The weather didn't pencil itself into your busy schedule?

Me: Fuck off.

Bastian: Oh shit, are you firing Mother Nature?

Me: No, but I might fire your ass.

Bastian: As if.

I sigh and head into my bathroom to get dressed for my workout. Bastian knows damn well that his job is safe. And I hate that I fucking care about the prick. He's somehow weaseled his way into my cold, dead heart.

I have just enough time for a run and to feed the dogs before my first meeting in the morning. I brush my teeth and toss on my gym clothes before heading down the hall.

Normally, my dogs come running, demanding that I feed them, but I'm greeted in the east wing by more silence. I decide to get a mile run in along with my circuit training before I attempt to find my dogs. If they aren't looking for me, then I'm sure they are fine. When I asked for guard dogs for the property, I definitely thought of scarier ones than Ames and Isaac. They basically act like two overgrown puppies who enjoy naps and playtime.

I contemplate what Ms. Garren is doing while I run. Did she get up already? Did she find the kitchen? She certainly didn't leave, because I set the alarm, but also, she'd have nowhere to go with the three feet of snow piling up outside.

As I finish running and start lifting weights, I ponder if she'll have to stay longer than today. The weather forecast called for snow through tomorrow. That means it could be at least two more days before the plows get out here. My estate is off a side road that is plowed by the county, but my drive is privately plowed. However, the guy we hire to plow the drive won't be able to get out here until that side road is plowed. Fuck.

There was one other blizzard years ago and we got stuck out here for almost a week. But surely, this storm won't be as bad.

I finish my reps and grab a towel and water. As I walk out of the gym, I glance in the direction of the guest room. Curiosity gets the better of me and I find myself walking toward the room. I take a deep breath and decide to knock on the door and offer her coffee. I can be a host. I can be kind.

Tap. Tap. Tap.

I hear nothing on the other side. This time I knock louder.

TAP. TAP. TAP.

Still nothing. What in the hell?

I slowly turn the doorknob on the right-side door and open it, peering inside. All three dogs are lying on the bed.

They raise their heads, stare at me, and then lay their heads back down as if I'm the least interesting thing they've ever seen.

What. The. Fuck?

"Ms. Garren?" I ask.

I step inside and turn to the right.

Christ!

Isabelle Garren is standing at the bathroom door naked. A towel in her hand. Her eyes lift from the towel to mine and she gives a barely audible squeak before quickly clutching the towel to her chest. But it's too late. I've seen her...all of her...and she is absolutely gorgeous. A painter or sculptor couldn't have made a more perfect woman. Her curves, her pale skin, even a cute little heart-shaped birth-mark on the right side of her abdomen. I admit, I'm a little surprised to find she shaves or waxes...everywhere. In my head, I envisioned some full-bushed, spinster librarian who hadn't thought to bother with such frivolous societal expec-tations.

I spin around and face the other way.

"I'm sorry...I knocked and thought you might have gone downstairs," I explain.

I hear the rustling of what I assume is clothing.

"I—I was just going to feed the d-dogs," she stammers, clearly embarrassed.

Fuck. For some unknown reason, I feel bad, and I *never* feel bad.

"I am sorry. I'll feed the dogs so you can get dressed. If you haven't checked outside yet, I'm afraid to inform you that the weather has gotten worse overnight. I don't think you'll be leaving until at least tomorrow," I explain.

I hear the curtains move and then natural light streams into the room.

"Oh, shit," she mutters under her breath.

"Yeah...oh, shit," I repeat. I look over at the dogs. "Come on, boys."

Ames pops his head up again and cocks it to one side as if considering my request.

"Food," I state sternly.

Isaac jumps off the bed and Ames and what was her dog's name again? Well, in either case, those two follow Isaac and I lead them out of the room.

"There's breakfast in the kitchen," I add as I shut her door, giving her some privacy, but not before I glance over my shoulder. She's standing in front of the bay window staring out at the blizzard while towel-drying her hair. She seems almost oblivious to my existence or perhaps she's still too embarrassed to look at me.

The three dogs follow me to the kitchen and sit in front of empty food bowls. I start opening cupboards trying to find a third bowl that can be used by my guest's canine.

I look at my dogs. "You know you two are fucking traders, right?" I ask them.

Isaac gives me a goofy look with his tongue hanging out. At least Ames has the wherewithal to look slightly sheepish.

I find the food container and throw some food into their bowls and some metal bowl I'm fairly certain is for some kind of food preparation.

The dog doesn't move as mine begin to eat.

"You can eat," I tell it. It stares at me.

"Food?" I restate.

I point to the bowl. "Food."

The dog just looks at the bowl and back at me but doesn't budge.

"Uh, buddy, I'm not sure what's happening here. Aren't you hungry?" I ask him. I pat his head and he leans into my touch.

He's a sweet beast. "You're a good boy, aren't you?" I say as

I feel the silky fur of his ears. "I bet you could teach these goofs a thing or two, huh?"

I swear this dog's eyes look into my soul.

I lean down a little, so we are nose to nose. "I'm at a loss here, friend. What do I need to do for you to eat? Do you not like the food?" I ask him as I scratch behind his right ear.

I hear something from the doorway, and I look up to find Isabelle leaning against the doorjamb.

She's giving me a curious look. Unlike yesterday when she was dressed in an outfit that screamed librarian, today her hair is down in soft curls around her face and she's wearing sweatpants, a hoodie, and running shoes. Only I now know what lies beneath those clothes and I can't unsee it. She can try all she likes to cover up, but shit, she has a body for sin under all of that. I give my head a little shake. I need to clear those thoughts immediately. I am apparently in need of a booty call with one of my regular go-to flings in the city because it's been too long and this irritating woman standing in front of me is definitely not my type.

"Eat it all up, Felipe," she says without breaking eye contact.

I furrow my brows. What the hell is she...oh, the dog. It's a dog command. I hear Felipe eating and look down to see him enjoying his breakfast alongside my dogs who are nearly finished.

I walk over to the freezer, opening the giant stainless-steel door, I peruse the breakfast options. I settle on a quiche. I pop it in the microwave and use the instructions left on it to reheat it.

"There's food...in there," I say as I motion to the freezer.

I turn when I don't hear her reply. She's sitting on a stool in the corner of the kitchen watching me.

"Help yourself," I add as the microwave beeps. I remove

my quiche and set it on the counter. She doesn't get up and I study her. She's watching me, watching her.

"Do you need anything?" I ask. I'm not one to miss things but she's making me feel like I am. It's irritating.

"Nope. I have some pastries that I brought and I'll just grab a coffee..." She trails off as she looks around the kitchen. She eyes the cappuccino maker and I watch as she finds the coffee beans and goes about making herself a drink. I want to ask how she knows her way around such a complicated kitchen device, but I refrain. She grabs a bag off the counter and a plate and sets out a tray of cookies and pastries from a bag that I hadn't even noticed. Spinning around, we come face-to-face. She looks up at me from beneath her thick lashes and something inside me stirs. I fight the sudden urge to take her face in my hands and kiss the ever-loving hell out of her.

I frown at that thought. Why would I even think that? Clearing my throat, I take a step back, putting much-needed space between us. I look down at the tray. "Where did those come from?"

"My friend owns the bakery in town. You should try one. They are her specialty," she explains as she motions to a cookie.

"Maybe later. I have a call," I state as I stuff a few more bites in my mouth before heading out of the kitchen. I need to put space between us. I should be more irritated than I am with having an unexpected houseguest. I shouldn't find her intriguing or charming at all. I feel my jaw clenching at my annoyance with myself as I slam my office door and take my seat at my desk. A long morning of conference calls will help clear my head and put my mind back on my work, where it should be.

CHAPTER SIX

Isa

So much for Elisha's cookies wooing my host. I grab an oatmeal raisin and take a bite as I lean on the counter. Felipe comes over and nuzzles my elbow.

"Hey, buddy," I mutter absentmindedly as I stroke his head with my free hand. I finish the cookie and my cappuccino. I clean up but leave the tray of cookies on the counter. Maybe Mr. Grumpykins will change his mind later.

His behavior is giving me whiplash. First, he was a total dick. Then, he turned into some overprotective weirdo. Then, well, he saw me naked...that was embarrassing. But shit, the way his eyes darkened as he took me in all while wearing nothing but gym shorts was hot as fuck. Then, he was all cold again. But the way he spoke to Felipe...does he have some soft side to him? Or maybe he's one of those stereotypical rich people who only show affection to dogs and horses? And now, he's holed up in that office of his.

I check the time on my phone and notice that I have zero

bars. I frown. Hopefully, it's just the storm and I'll get them back later. Sighing, I turn to Felipe.

"I guess it's just you and me. Let's go explore this place," I state as I walk into the hallway. Adam had pointed out a few rooms last night, but I don't really remember them. Didn't he motion toward the library? I try to retrace our steps. After getting lost three times, I find a long hallway in the back of the house...or at least I think it's the back of the house, between the blinding snow falling outside and my disorientation inside this maze of opulence, I'm not totally sure.

I'm greeted at the end of the hall by double doors that are easily fifteen feet high. They look old, much older than the house. I run my hands over the intricate carvings on the doors.

"Shall we?" I ask Felipe. He wags his tail.

I push on one of the doors and gasp as it opens. I don't move, aside from reaching to my right where I see light switches. I turn them on one by one and I just stare. I'm in the library. It's the most beautiful library I've ever seen in person. It's three stories tall. There's a mural painted on the ceiling. Dark mahogany wood shelves line every wall. There are at least seven of those sliding ladders against brass railings that run along the top of the bookshelves. A section of the shelves on the second floor has glass-front doors. Two of them look to have locks. I momentarily ponder if the books I so desperately need are inside. There are beautiful green-glass lamps throughout the space, but the shelves also are backlit and appear to have lights embedded into the tops of them so that you can easily read the spines of the books. Several spaces in between shelves have giant paintings hanging from them with special lighting overhead. One of them looks like a family painting of Adam with his parents. I examine it. He appears to be a teenager, but those blue eyes are still the same. They are his mother's eyes. But his hair is most definitely the same color as his father's. In addition to the one family painting, there are several of cardinals. I wonder why as I look at each one.

My gaze travels from the paintings to the three windows running the height of the room on the back wall. Some of the windowpanes are made of stained glass and the light from the snowstorm leaves colorful patterns on the floor.

The floor is a checkered marble pattern, but instead of marble, it's dark and light wood, giving it a cozy feeling. To the far end of the room, there is an alcove that is only one story high. There are two desks and four oversized chairs with ottomans. Against the wall where I entered is a fireplace with two more chairs and a sofa in front of it along with a coffee table that has newspapers and magazines on it. The few areas of the wall without wood shelves are painted a greenish blue that complements the light fixtures or maybe the light fixtures complement the walls? I'm definitely no interior designer.

I see a phone tucked into one of the alcove desks. I frown and wonder if it works. Maybe I can call my parents from it.

I walk over and pick up the receiver. There is only static on the other end. I haven't used a phone this old in a long time. I press the button where the handset sits and release it, but still no dial tone. I hang up and walk back to the door. Perhaps the phone or computer in Adam's office works. I could call or email from there. I go to open the door when suddenly it's pushed toward me.

I yelp and sway backward as I lose my footing. I reach out behind me hoping to break my fall, but I'm suddenly stopped. My eyes look up and focus on a worried face staring down at me. Adam.

"Are you OK?" he asks, his eyes searching mine. His hands are gripping my waist. I blush under his scrutiny.

"Yes. Thank you. I...you surprised me," I stammer as he

helps me to stand. His hands remain on my waist for a moment longer than they need to, but oddly I miss his touch when he releases me. We're so close. I can feel his breath against my forehead and smell his cologne. He hadn't been wearing that for his workout this morning. As if sensing our unusual proximity, he slowly steps back, giving me space.

I look into his eyes wondering why he's here. I don't have to wait long for my answer.

"The phone lines aren't working and my Wi-Fi is down," he explains.

I purse my lips as I consider what he's said. I guess I'm not calling anyone.

I hold up my phone and show him that I have no reception.

He nods. "Me either. Sometimes when it's storming the nearest tower doesn't work. Hopefully, it's just the storm and it doesn't need repairs. As for my phones, they should be up and running unless..." He pauses as if a new thought has interrupted him. He doesn't continue but walks across the large room and peers out one of the enormous windows.

A loud sigh echoes in the otherwise silent space. "Well, that's fucking fantastic," he groans.

I take large strides as I cross the room to stand next to him. Through the near-whiteout conditions, I can just barely make out a tree that's been uprooted not far from the house-slash-billionaire-lair, and with it, I can just barely see some black lines poking in and around the roots.

"I'm guessing that those cables are for your phone and Wi-Fi?" I ask.

He nods as he stares into the white abyss of his backyard. Can you really call it a backyard if it's several acres large? Well, whatever you would call it, grounds or property, it's going to need a lot of work after this storm. I can't see all of it with the snow falling but I can make out at least two other downed trees.

"Want a drink?" he asks.

My eyebrow rise. "It's like ten in the morning," I state.

He shrugs. "Well, I can't work. I can't even make contact with the outside world. So..." He trails off as he glances over at me. He looks lost as if without work, he doesn't know how to live. Strange.

I let out a long breath. "Fuck it. OK," I agree to this truce of sorts, or at least that's what it feels like he's offering me.

He walks over to a small cabinet that I hadn't yet noticed. It's built into the alcove in the same dark wood as the shelves. He pulls two tumblers from inside the glass cabinet and grabs a bottle of Scottish whiskey from a row of bottles against the back of the counter space. He pours us both a glass and holds one out to me. I accept it with a whispered, "Thank you."

He doesn't wait for me to offer a toast, nor does he offer one. He merely gulps the two fingers of liquid in a single swallow and goes back to pour himself another. Clearly, having no contact with the outside world is bothering this man, which I find ironic since he seems to be some sort of recluse out here.

"How long do you think the cell service will be down?" I ask.

He shrugs. "No idea. Why? Do you need to call someone?"

I lean against one of the chairs. "Not really. I just wanted to let my parents know that I'm alright. Hopefully, my text messages went through last night."

He pauses when I say "parents."

"Are you close to your...parents?" he asks. This time he slowly sips the amber drink in his tumbler.

"I am. They live close by. They're my biggest supporters," I explain.

"What do they do?" he asks, and I'm surprised he's asking, as if I just unlocked a secret caring part of this otherwise cold, billionaire asshole...well, aside from his obvious love of dogs.

"My dad owns his own company. He invented a specialized temperature gauge for indoor heating. My mom paints, but mostly she helps my dad with business stuff. They recently sold his company to a larger one. They are starting to wind down and retire. They both love cruises and want to go on more," I babble on and then promptly stop, realizing that I'm oversharing. I tend to do that.

"That's nice. I take it his company has done well?" Adam inquires, but it sounds more like he's mulling over a business proposition.

"It has," I reply. I decide to leave out how much Dad has made. I could have access to the trust fund he set up, hell, he could help the library, if I let him. My parents may not know how bad things are there. I just want to do this one thing on my own, without their help. It's silly, and I guess if borrowing Adam's book collection doesn't work out, then I'll change my tune, but for now, my pride has gotten the better of me. I glance over at his family portrait. I know his parents were killed in a car accident. He was the sole survivor that day. I look back at him, his gaze had followed mine and he's still looking at his parents. A small part of me begins to feel a little sorry for him. He was quite young when they died, only just out of college. I was a teenager, but even I had heard the news of the famous local family.

"They were very good-looking," I say, my voice barely above a whisper.

"Do you play chess?" Adam asks, completely changing the topic.

My eyes widen and I stare up at him. "Sorry, what?" I ask as I process that he won't or can't talk about his parents. I search his eyes and watch as he shuts down any emotion he might be feeling. I can't imagine losing my parents, and from his reaction, I can't help but wonder if he was very close to them. He had to have been. Why else would he shut down a discussion about them? Something about this makes me want to hug him, but I refrain.

"Chess?" he asks as he motions behind me. I swivel to see a chessboard pattern on the small side table in between the two chairs in the alcove.

"Oh, uh, sort of," I stammer.

His lips twitch a little in that now familiar fight to not smile. I wonder what a true smile would look like on him if we cleared away some of that beard and trimmed his hair a bit. He's hiding under all of it, but even with that mask, I know he's good-looking. His portrait made that quite obvious.

The lights choose this moment to flicker once and then go dark.

"Shit," Adam mutters.

The only light now streams in from the large windows but the "L" shape of the room and the windowless alcove make it dark where we are.

"Stay still. Let me light the fire for us," he says. I nod in his direction as I watch his shadowed figure head to the stone fireplace.

A moment later, it's on. It's a gaslit fireplace and turns on with a flip of a switch.

"Good thing the tree didn't uproot a gas line," I mumble to myself.

Adam glares at me. "Not funny," he hisses.

I shrug and fight a smile.

He picks up the side table and places it between the chairs near the fireplace. I take a seat and he opens a drawer in the table and begins to place the chess pieces on the board.

"I'm guessing that you're quite good at this game?" I ask.

"I'm not going to win any tournaments, but I can hold my own," he replies as he leans back and places his right ankle on his left knee. He brings his tumbler to his lips, and I have to remind myself to breathe. This man looks like something in one of those billionaire alpha books in the romance section of the library. He's even wearing a three-piece suit, although he's taken off his jacket and his sleeves are rolled up, which only makes him look sexier. Sexier? No, that's not right. He's...domineering...or something. I would never be attracted to someone so...so...pompous.

"You may go first," he urges as he motions to the board with a single finger.

I study the pieces and make my move. A pawn.

"You sure about that?" he asks.

Here we go.

"I am," I say. What Mr. Adam Wellington doesn't know, is that I am more than just alright at this game. My grandfather loved chess, and when I'd go visit him in his little mountain cabin every summer, we'd spend hours playing.

Adam moves a pawn. I raise an eyebrow.

"And so it begins," I whisper with a wink.

Something appearing to be close to a smile tugs on the corners of his lips. But he quickly squashes the feeling, bringing his glass back up to sip more whiskey.

"A question for a move," I suggest. I suddenly have the overwhelming urge to get to know this man. After all, he's seen me butt-ass naked, so why keep any secrets now?

His eyebrow rises a bit. "Fine, but I may not answer your questions."

"Fair. Same," I retort.

I move another pawn, setting my trap for him. He stares at me, waiting for my question.

"Why do you never come to town?" I ask.

"I'm a busy man, Ms. Garren," he replies as he reaches down and moves his knight. Novice move, Mr. Wellington.

"Why are you so adamant that you need *my* book collection?" he asks.

I tap my cheek, pretending to need time to contemplate my next move. "Isa...please. Because it's the best one. You're a local and your ancestor provided the building space for the library many years ago. I think that adds something of value to the exhibit," I state as I move my rook.

"Do you always stay at this property?" I ask.

"No. I have a home in the city. When I have board meetings or such, I stay there," he answers as he moves his rook.

I don't take his bait. I move my queen and he seems surprised based on the small tic of his jaw. I've caught him off guard and something about that pleases me immensely, as if pressing this man's buttons is my new favorite hobby.

This time, he does pause to consider his move. When he makes it, I smile. This game won't be long.

"If your father owns a company, why are you bothering with a grant? Just ask him," he states. I'm both shocked he just said that and also surprised at his insights.

After weighing my answers, I settle on the truth for some unknown reason. "Pride," I admit as I move a pawn, revealing my strategy to him.

"Well, well, well, someone understated her chess abilities," he murmurs as he stares at the board, knowing he's going to lose. I have a sneaking suspicion that Mr. Wellington doesn't lose often.

He makes a feeble attempt to stop my play. His eyes don't leave mine as he places his piece on a new square. My face begins to flush under his intense gaze.

"You're braver than you like to admit. Why do you hide it?" he asks.

My face goes from pink to red as I process his words.

"I don't," I state as I move my queen. "Checkmate."

With a single, thick finger, he topples over his king.

"You're kinder than you like to admit. Why do you hide it?" I retort.

"I'm not kind," he says as he stands. "I should go light some fires in the other rooms to keep the house warm. We should have kept that old gas furnace," he mutters as he leaves me sitting alone in the library with a million more unanswered questions to ask.

CHAPTER SEVEN

Adam

I go room to room turning on fireplaces to keep the building warm. As I turn a corner, I hear noises in the kitchen.

I slowly open the door and find Isa chopping veggies by candlelight. A giant pot sits on the gas stove.

"What are you doing?" I ask.

"Making soup," she answers without looking up.

"Why?" I ask.

Her eyes meet mine. "Because...it sounded good and the gas lines work, so might as well cook real food."

"But...Mrs. Potter has meals in the freezer," I point out.

"The power is out," she says as if I'm an idiot. She sighs. "I don't want to keep opening the freezer door because I don't know how long the power will be out. These veggies were all in the basket over there."

"No meat?" I ask, already questioning her soup.

She rolls her eyes and I narrow mine. "There are lentils in it. Don't worry, you'll get your protein."

"You didn't ask if I was allergic to anything," I point out.

She stops mid-chop. "Are you allergic to anything?"

"No."

She points a knife at me. "Then, why are you asking me to ask you that? You're a real grump, you know that?"

I laugh sarcastically. "Right. Anyhow..." I trail off as a memory of my mom cooking soup in this kitchen comes barreling into my mind out of nowhere. I'd forgotten about that day. It wasn't much different than today. A snow day from school. My mom telling Mrs. Potter to stay home.

Isa stops her chopping and walks around the peninsula. Her hand reaches for my forearm.

"Adam? Are you alright?" she asks, her voice gentle and calming like a balm on my soul.

I take a deep breath. "I'm fine." For reasons I can't explain I decide I want to help.

"Can I help?"

Her smile makes me want to do the right thing, whatever that is. It makes me want to please her again. It makes me want to keep doing things so she's always smiling.

"Absolutely," she replies as her hand slides down my arm, and she entwines her fingers with mine, giving a small tug. "Come on."

I let her guide me around the counter. She motions to the knife and vegetables. "Chop those up and toss them in the pot." I give her a look. I suppose I'm not used to people demanding things of me. She pauses and her lips twitch with another smile. "Please," she adds. I nod my understanding and get to work.

She begins adding spices and herbs to the pot. We each complete our tasks in silence, but it's a comfortable silence as if we've known each other for years. There are a few moments where we both turn and end up face-to-face and I swear I hear her sharp intake of breath over the liquid bubbling on the stove. Could she be affected by me just as I am toward her? She seems too pure, too innocent, and much too kind. She deserves someone better, someone...undamaged.

When she finally puts the lid on the pot to simmer the soup, she asks, "What now?"

"Now?" I ask.

"Yeah, we have all day...or at least all evening," she explains.

Right. I'm a host now to a guest stuck in my home.

"You're not very good at this hosting thing, are you?" she asks.

"I didn't ask for guests," I grumble under my breath.

"Well, sorry for getting stuck in your home. I wish I was in my own home, but I'm here. And based on that snow, I don't think I'm going anywhere," she states, motioning toward the door outside.

I swallow. I'm being a prick. My mother would kill me for acting this way.

"I..." I choke over the words, clearing my throat because apologies aren't something I'm accustomed to making. "You were in the library earlier. Do you want to see my collection?"

A smile lights up her face and she nods enthusiastically.

"Come on," I say as I motion for her to go through the door I open.

She follows me, and when we get to the library doors, she pauses and runs a finger over the door. "These doors are beautiful."

I smile at the memory of Dad finding them. I run my finger over the carvings, right alongside hers. Our fingers brush for a moment and neither of us pulls away.

"My father found these in an old manor house that was being renovated. The owner was changing the opening and was willing to sell them as they didn't have a place for them any longer. So Dad had them shipped here and we redid this entire room," I start. An unexpected laugh escapes me at the memory. "After he found these doors, he became super obsessed with finding reclaimed wood for the entire library. The shelves were from an old school in Scotland. The beams are from a church in France. The desks are from another school in Ireland. He spent that summer traveling as much as he could like he was on a quest or something."

That beautiful smile graces Isa's face again. "Your father sounds like a fun guy and I love that he went on a quest to find this library and put it all together here," she says as she looks around the room with such a sense of awe that I follow her gaze. It's like seeing it again for the first time.

"She loved cardinals," I say quietly as I look at the set of three paintings my mother won at an art auction.

"Your mom?" Isa asks.

I nod. "Her grandmother collected them and she started to gift them to Mom. It became their thing. Her grandmother said something about coming back as a cardinal and so Mom always stopped and talked to them when we'd go for walks. I used to tease her about it. She'd just smile and say *you'll understand someday. Maybe I'll come back as a cardinal.*"

I pause, feeling the weight of that moment like a ton of bricks on my chest.

Isa's reassuring hand reaches out and laces her fingers through mine again. "Your parents sound like amazing people."

"They were, but they were busy people too. Charity events and galas. They had an empire to run, an empire they inherited, just as I inherited it. I guess I never really understood the albatross it was until it was strapped around my own neck," I muse as I run a thumb along Isa's smooth skin. She doesn't pull away as if knowing her touch is providing me strength I didn't even know I needed.

With her hand still tucked in mine, I walk us up the main

staircase to the second floor and straight to the locked cabinets. These cabinets, while trimmed with mahogany, are fitted with fireproof glass and walls to protect the valuable books inside. Books passed down from my grandfather to my father and now to me.

I release Isa's hand and press my thumb to the lock. It looks old, but it's quite modern. The locks click and I open the door. I pull out a small drawer with special gloves inside and put on a pair while handing another pair to Isa who obliges. Then I pull out a first-edition copy of *Pride of Prejudice* and lay it out on a small tabletop that I pull out from its place tucked into the shelf.

Isa's fingers hesitate over the antique pages.

"You can touch it," I urge.

Her gloved finger runs over the words on the page. "It's amazing."

She looks at all the other books. *Moby Dick. Oliver Twist. Frankenstein.* And so many more.

"How did your grandfather end up with this collection?" she asks.

I give a sad smile. "His wife, my grandmother, loved books. When she got sick, he wanted to make her happy, so he began adding to the small collection she had started. And soon, there were twenty-eight priceless first editions of some of the most-read classics ever written. After she passed away, he would buy a single one each year on her birthday and leave it on the shelf with a red bow around it."

I know when Isa finds them. There are six of them, one for each year he lived past her death, and they still are wrapped with red satin bows.

A tear trails down Isa's cheek and I can't help myself. I reach out and wipe it away.

"That's beautiful," she says quietly as she quickly removes her gloves and wipes at her tears.

"I suppose it is. Theirs was a true love story. I mean my parents loved each other, but my grandparents' love was the stuff written in these books," I explain.

Isa sniffles and then giggles.

"What's so funny?" I ask.

"No, it's not...I'm sorry. I don't mean to laugh, it's just...I didn't picture you as a romantic, not even a little bit," she says with a lopsided grin on her face.

I shrug. "I'm not sure I'm a romantic, but I did love my family."

Out of nowhere, Isa suddenly wraps her arms around my waist and hugs me. "Thank you for sharing this with me," she says, her voice muffled against my chest.

I'm so shocked by her touch that I don't move for a long moment, but she doesn't back away, only grips me harder. Eventually, my arms wrap around her. It feels awkward at first, hugging another person after such a long time, but then it's like a dam breaks inside me, and I long for more of this. How long had it been since a human touched me like this? I'd had some flings with women over the past few years, but it wasn't intimate like this. How can this woman I've only known for twenty-four hours break through the wall I've built around my heart this quickly?

She pulls back a little and we stare at each other. My desire to kiss her overwhelms me this time and I begin to tilt my head down toward her lips. Her eyes start to close. My hands grip her backside and presses her body against mine.

"Chirp. Chirp. Chirp." My phone's bird ringtone might as well be a bucket of ice on us. We both jump back like we've touched a live wire.

"Your phone!" Isa exclaims.

"My phone!" I state at the same time. I pull it from my pocket. There's one bar but it's ringing. I groan because I know who it is even before I look at the screen. Bastian. That motherfucker is the worst wingman in the history of wing-men. Fine, that's a lie, but he just killed this moment.

I answer.

"Bastian, this better be important," I growl as I pick up the phone, putting it on speaker. I watch Isa bite her bottom lip in an attempt to stop her grin. Fuck, she's adorable and I want nothing more than to toss this phone over the balcony and kiss those lips. Bastian better be calling with the most crucial piece of information in the history of information.

"I...storm...maybe...need...later...Max..." Bastian's voice breaks up and I can't understand a damn thing he's saying.

"What?" I yell. Isa steps away, and I watch as she walks back down to the lower level of the library.

"The cell tower...fuck...call later..." Bastian's voice breaks up again and then the call drops and I'm left with static.

"Great," I mumble, hoping my friend is fine.

"You know Max Montgomery?" Isa's voice calls out from below.

"I do," I reply, wondering how she knows the owner of the best restaurant in town who also happens to be dating Bastian.

"Max's restaurant has the best ravioli in town. Do you play any games besides chess?" she calls out, changing the subject. She's not wrong about that ravioli. Bastian sometimes picks it up for me on his way out here.

I lean over the railing to see she's found a stash of board games in the cupboard.

I shrug. "It's been years."

She looks out the windows and then pulls out Monopoly. The dogs have already taken up residence next to the chairs in front of the fireplace as if they know this is where we need to be for the remainder of the day. Traitors.

"No way, that'll take all night," I state.

She grins. "Exactly."

I groan. Even her choice of games is infuriating. But with that hopeful smile on her face, I can't say "no." I'm beginning to think this woman has some sort of ancient magic power because I don't cave to other people...ever. But what she doesn't have is amazing business and strategy skills. She's definitely going to lose.

CHAPTER EIGHT

Isa

The knocking at the door wakes me and the dogs.

"Felipe!" I yelp as he steps on my foot. His barked response gets Ames and Isaac barking. Suddenly, the door flies open, and I'm greeted by a very worried-looking Adam. His eyes search the room as though he's about to find an intruder here to murder me.

"What's going on?" he asks, his eyes still scanning everything.

I prop myself up on my elbows and stare at him. "I don't know. You tell me. One of us was sleeping five seconds ago."

He pauses and his gaze drops and that's when I realize my boobs and tank top have rearranged themselves in my slumber. I quickly adjust the top.

He doesn't look away from me. Does this man have no shame? I search his eyes which are still fixated on my now perky nipples. Nope. Definitely none.

"My eyes are up here," I mumble, motioning to my eyes as

I toss back the giant duvet and climb out of bed using the step stool. The dogs, on the other hand, are unphased by the bed's height and jump off as if the ground is a mere foot away.

"Are you hungry?" Adam asks, finally removing his fixation from my breasts to my eyes.

It takes every muscle in my body to keep my mouth from forming the suggestive words, "Are you?" What the fuck is wrong with me? One day with this alphahole and I'm having sexual fantasies. I swear we almost kissed last night until Bastian's call. Too bad the signal went down again after that.

I walk over to the window and throw open the curtains. I can make out more of the grounds today. The snow is still falling but it's not a complete whiteout.

"I think you might be stuck here for another day or two. Although I did manage to get our backup generators going this morning," Adam says, his breath on my back. I nearly jump at his closeness. He must be reaching for a light switch because a second later he turns it on, and the room lights up behind me.

Turning around, I come face-to-chest with the beast of a man. He's been working out again based on his attire and his bare chest. A towel is slung over his shoulder, and I watch beads of sweat as they run down his pectoral muscles.

"Eyes up here," he says with a smirk. My gaze shoots up to his face. He's smiling. Like an actual smile. Huh. It looks good on him.

I cross my arms and glare at him, which has the opposite effect because his smile only widens.

"You're infuriating," I mumble.

He laughs. This man actually has the audacity to laugh. "Takes one to know one, I suppose," he says as he steps to the side and looks out the window. I look up at him again. He's changed somehow in the past two days. Last night was...fun, after the initial awkwardness of what I thought was an almost kiss. I wasn't sure if Adam was going to stay, but then he did. That was unexpected. We played board games until late into the evening and then went into the kitchen rifling for snacks. He ate peanut butter right out of the jar and then shared his spoon with the dogs. I announced he was disgusting. He declared me a bad canine friend. Somehow, that ended in a food fight. And I swear as we cleaned up and washed up the dishes in the sink, he had leaned down again to kiss me...or I had hoped he was going to kiss me until Felipe jumped between us and started drinking out of the faucet. Why do I want this man to kiss me so badly? I need one of my friends here to tell me I've lost my mind. Perhaps I've spent too many hours reading books in the romance section. I should switch to fantasy or thrillers.

"Do you have any fantasy books in that library of yours?" I ask, deciding now is as good a time as any to start shifting my mindset, especially when a half-naked Adam is standing next to me.

Adam turns quickly, his eyes wide. "You like fantasy books?"

I shrug. "I'm...just getting into the genre," I half lie. Then with a tilt of my head, I feel my curiosity getting the better of me. "Do you like it?"

His grin returns, and for some reason, I want to keep doing things to keep it on his face. I want to see him happy. Happy Adam is fun and playful, unlike Curmudgeon Adam, who's a dick.

"Love it. Hey, we could watch some sci-fi films today. I haven't been down to the theater in forever," he says with a hint of excitement in his voice.

"I'm sorry...what?" I ask as I motion to the window. "We can't go to the theater. It's probably closed."

He laughs. "We don't have to *go* anywhere. I have one here. And since we have power again, we can use it."

I roll my eyes. "Of course, you do." I look over at the dogs. They are sitting neatly in a row of three, clearly waiting for someone to feed them. "Fine. You feed those beasts and I'll grab a shower."

"Beasts?" he says in mock horror. "I see nothing but angelic sweet creatures here."

The dogs wag their tails happily. I roll my eyes again.

"Fine, just one beast here," I tease as I poke his chest which may as well be carved from marble because aside from his smooth skin, that muscle is as hard as a rock. I pull my finger quickly away and turn to cover the blush creeping up my neck. "See you in the kitchen," I manage as I grab my last clean clothes from my gym bag and head into the bathroom.

I take my time showering and shaving and trying out every oil, lotion, and soap available in the bathroom because why the hell not? By the time I finish, I smell clean, and my skin feels amazing. Maybe staying here hasn't been the worst thing ever.

I head down to the kitchen and am surprised to see Adam dressed, showered, and cooking. Just like after his workouts, he has a towel draped over his shoulder. He's humming to himself. The dogs are chewing on something while lying around him.

"What are they eating?" I ask as I reach down to see that Felipe has a carrot lodged between his paws and is making small bites into it like it's baby corn.

"Carrots," Adam says. "I hope you like omelets."

"I do," I reply as I set to work on a cappuccino. "Want one?" I ask him.

"Sure."

We work in silence, both setting things on a small island where there are two stools.

"Fuck it," he says as he turns off the stove and looks at the island. "Grab your drink and plate. We're going to the dining room."

I raise my eyebrows. "Like...a formal one?"

He nods and I follow him. The dogs are too infatuated with their carrots to bother coming with us. We walk through two sets of doors and enter a giant two-story room. There's a table in the middle that could easily seat twenty people.

"Uh, that's a lot of table," I declare as I look around, unsure of where to put my things. I watch Adam hesitate at the head of the table but then he places his things there and pulls out the seat along the side closest to his chair. He motions for me to sit. I place my things down and comply.

He pushes in my chair and walks to a long table behind us. It's made of inlaid wood with intricate patterns and I'm sure it's worth something ridiculous. He grabs linens and silverware...actual "silver" ware.

He places the linen in my lap and the silverware on either side of my plate.

"Fancy," I mutter.

He chuckles. "I haven't been in here in..." He trails off and I swear I see sadness on his face. "Well, in a really long time. It's silly not to use it when I have company."

"I wouldn't even know what to do with all these rooms," I say, taking a bite. I groan as the delicious flavors hit my taste buds. "Holy shit, this is actually good," I mumble after swallowing.

"I took a cooking class in France a while back," he says. A distant look clouds his face, and when he sees I'm watching, he clears his throat. "That's where I met Bastian."

"I think he mentioned that once. It's where he's from, right?" I ask, using my limited knowledge of Bastian to further the conversation because now, I'm curious.

"Yes. I...was unhappy and was at this bar all the time. Bastian was the bartender there. But during the days, he worked as a sous chef. The chef he worked with offered me some cooking classes after I ate there a few times and commented about how I wished I could cook French cuisine."

"How did Bastian end up here?" I ask when I really want to ask why he was unhappy, but decide I should tread lightly.

Adam laughs at the memory. "I...I was unhappy after a breakup and so was Bastian. We bonded over our hatred of love as one does after a breakup. We became good friends. Bastian needed a change. I had to come home, and so I offered him a job here." He pauses again and laughs.

"What?"

"He may have come along on one condition." Adam pauses and smiles. "I don't get to make any requests. He gets to choose the menu."

"And you agreed to that?" I ask, utterly shocked.

He shrugs. "I gave him a list of things I won't eat. And told him to have at it."

"This is shocking. You seem like such a..." I trail off and bite my lower lip.

"Such a what?" he asks, raising an eyebrow.

I blush. "A...control freak."

He laughs and sets his fork down. "Wow. Two days into knowing me and you already have me pegged as a control freak."

"I mean, if the shoe fits," I mutter.

He laughs some more. "I like what I like."

"Clearly," I reply with a roll of my eyes.

I look around the room again. There are a few giant paintings, including another one of a cardinal. There are even a few books on a table.

"How come those aren't in the library?" I ask, pointing at them with my fork.

Adam looks over and shrugs. "My dad loved having a book to read at breakfast. So, he used to keep a few in here."

I squint to read the spines and giggle. "They are all action-adventure books."

"That was his favorite genre," Adam explains.

"But I see one fantasy novel," I point out.

I swear I see Adam's cheeks turn a little pink. "That one is mine."

I grin. I like this side of him.

I finish my breakfast and Adam reaches for my plate. I pull it back. "Nope. You cooked. I'll clean," I say as I grab his plate. He helps me bring everything back into the kitchen where I wash the dishes and place them back in the cupboard.

"Come on, let's go watch some movies," he urges as he places his hand on the small of my back and guides me toward a different side door. I go through it, and he keeps guiding me down hallways and then to a door with a set of stairs leading downstairs.

I pause and turn. "Are you sure you aren't taking me to your dungeon?" I ask with a raised eyebrow.

His lips quirk a little. "Maybe."

"What type of dungeon is down there?" I ask coyly.

He leans forward so his lips brush the shell of my ear and I feel goose bumps rise on my arms. "Wouldn't you like to know?" he replies.

"It sounds dangerous," I whisper, playing along.

"A little danger can be fun," he responds. "Or are you...chicken?"

I roll my eyes. "One dungeon tour coming up," I state as I start down the steps. There are mazes of hallways down here and it does creep me out a little, but the door we want isn't far, and when I step inside and he turns on a light, I let out a gasp.

It's a full-on movie theater. Literal rows of seats, maybe five of them with a screen rolled down from the ceiling. It even has those red curtains on the other side of it. A projector hangs overhead, and I notice a small computer to our right.

"Let's start with a classic," he suggests, motioning to the seats.

I pick one near the middle as I look around the room. There's a popcorn machine to the left.

"Can we?" I ask, pointing to it.

"Huh?" Adam's voice comes from over by the computer.

"Make popcorn."

"Oh, uh, yeah, sure," he replies. I turn to look at him. He's completely fixated by the computer.

I get up and head over to the popcorn machine. It seems easy enough, and eventually, I figure it out. I stand in front of it, patiently waiting for my snack when I feel a presence behind me. Adam's giant hand reaches past my arm and grabs the scoop.

"You'll need this in a second," he says against my ear. What is it with this man sneaking up behind me? What he doesn't realize is that I've already scooped some of the popcorn into a bucket and am holding it in front of me, and when he startles me with his proximity and whispered words, my reflexes take over. Just as he finishes speaking, the popcorn in my hand goes flying and I let out a curse. It all happens in slow motion. Literal popcorn rains down on us and scatters all over the floor.

"Oh my God! I'm so sorry," I stammer as I get down on my knees trying to retrieve the kernels from the floor.

A film is starting to play on the screen but I'm too focused on finding the now ruined snack food to pay attention.

"Here, let me—" Adam starts, but my head is down, and I

don't realize he's already bending over to help me. I come up as he goes down and we collide, both of us falling in the process. He grabs me in a failed attempt to stop me from hitting the ground, and before I know it, he somehow ninja rolls and I'm lying down with him hovering over me.

"I...are you OK?" I ask as I look up at him while simultaneously rubbing my forehead that hit his chin, or at least I think it was his chin.

His eyes are looking at my forehead and he reaches out to run his thumb over it. "Are you alright?" he asks, his eyebrows furrowed.

"I'll live. I'm sorry. I'm sorry about all of this. I'm sure you'd rather be snowed in alone," I mutter. What a disaster! I should have just waited to come out here, but no, like an idiot, I got all hyped up from Elisha's speech and barreled out here with my take-no-prisoners attitude.

His hand slides down to my cheek and he cups my face. I realize he's doing all this while planking over me. Shit, this man is in some seriously good shape.

"I...I'm glad you're here. It's been...fun," he stumbles over his words as his eyes search mine.

I grin up at him. "Fun?"

"Yeah, fun."

"You're having *fun* with *me*?" I ask, pointing to my chest. Because I can't believe the Adam that I met two days ago has fun doing anything. That Adam had a giant stick up his ass, but this Adam...yeah, he's sort of fun.

His eyes travel down my face to my lips. And for reasons I can't explain to even myself, I want him to kiss me. I want this recluse, sweet-to-dogs-when-no-one-is-looking, omelet-cooking-extraordinaire, hot-as-hell, confusing-as-hell alpha-hole to kiss the hell out of me.

"Don't look at me like that, Isa. I only have so much

control," he mumbles, and I know he's not going to kiss me, and something in me snaps.

"Then don't have so much control," I counter.

His eyes snap from my lips. "You don't know what you're asking."

"I do know what I'm asking. Don't act like we didn't almost kiss at least three different times since I arrived here. Don't act like you didn't stare at my naked body with such lust that I thought I might burst into flames just from your gaze. And don't act like you haven't purposefully used any excuse to touch me, since I got here," I state not looking away from him because his face is so close that I can't look anywhere but at him even if I wanted to. "And furthermore—"

"You're driving me crazy! Shut the hell up and let me kiss you already," he growls as he cups my head in his hand and crashes his lips to mine.

Now, I've been kissed before. I'm no stranger to making out with a man, but this kiss...this kiss is unlike any other I've experienced. Adam Wellington kisses with his entire body and soul. For a man who rarely leaves his estate, he has most definitely not forgotten how to kiss. His lips apply the perfect pressure. His tongue grazes my lower lip, coaxing it open, but not as forcefully as I would have expected. Instead, it's almost like he's asking permission. And when I part my lips in acceptance, his tongue slides lazily against mine as though he's got all the time in the world. His beard scratches against my skin but something about that excites me. The thumb of his hand that's cupping my head, makes lazy circles against my neck, right below my ear. He tastes like coffee and a hint of mint. He moves his lips from mine and trails kisses along my jaw and down my neck, all while still holding himself up on one elbow. I let out a sound that's somewhere between a moan and a whimper.

I'm not sure how long we kiss...a minute or maybe two, but he's pulling back all too soon and my eyelids slide open to look at him.

"We're missing the film. Come on," he says as he gets to his feet and holds his hand out to mine. I'm confused as I take it, and he hoists me up as if I weigh nothing. He grabs the popcorn container and fills it up and goes to sit down, placing the container on the seat next to him. I frown as he motions for me to sit on the other side of the popcorn.

After a moment, I sit and stare up at the screen. *Close Encounters of the Third Kind.* Not the film I would have thought he'd pick. He grabs a handful of popcorn and eats it as if nothing has happened as if we didn't kiss at all. Maybe he should have put on *The Twilight Zone* because I feel like I've stepped right into that.

"I can hear you thinking all the way over here. Stop over-analyzing our kiss and watch the film, Isa," he says without turning to look at me.

I glare at him. "How do you do it?" I ask.

This time, he turns to look at me. "Do what?"

"Be so caring and kind one second and then a total...argh! You're so frustrating!" I whisper-yell because I can't help the fact that being quiet in a movie theater is engrained in my head even though we are the only ones in here.

He smirks. "You're equally infuriating."

I narrow my eyes even more. "I can't believe I kissed you."

He chuckles. "I think it was *me* who kissed you."

"Semantics," I mutter as I cross my arms and stare back at the screen.

A piece of popcorn flies in front of my face. Followed by another one. And another.

"Will you stop that? I'm trying to watch the movie," I say loudly.

I hear crunching to my left and I glance over to find the

dogs eating up the popcorn on the floor. Except Felipe, who is sitting three seats down from me with his mouth open. A piece of popcorn goes sailing through the air and he catches it in his mouth. It's actually quite impressive.

"Stop feeding him popcorn," I hiss, looking at Adam out of the corner of my eye.

He shrugs. "Sorry, Felipe. Your mother is a party pooper."

I roll my eyes and try to focus on the film for the next two hours. Eventually, I give in to eating the popcorn and reach for a handful as the movie comes to its dramatic ending. I feel Adam's hand in the popcorn container, and before I can grab a handful, he entwines his fingers with mine. I don't pull away. He squeezes my hand and I squeeze his back. I haven't a clue what we're communicating here, but I feel more connected to him in this moment than I have to even Elisha or my parents. It's unexpected and I'm not sure how to unpack whatever this feeling is.

The movie credits begin to roll, and I look over at Adam. He's not watching the screen. Instead, his eyes are fixed on my face.

Why is everything about him so intense?

Another movie begins. *Willow*. I giggle. "I haven't seen this movie in a very long time."

He grins. "Me either."

Then he looks more serious. "Can I ask you a question?"

I nod slowly, curious about what he wants to know.

"Why a librarian?"

I look down and watch our hands. His thumb is rubbing mine, back and forth.

"There's a lot of reasons," I say, dodging his question.

"Such as?"

I squirm in my seat. Truthfully, my parents are super outgoing people. They were always at meetings and selling their product. I was always a wallflower. My mom took me to story time at the library when I was about four years old. The librarian at the time, Mrs. Hatcher, was reading a fairy tale to a group of kids. I remember sitting down and becoming completely enchanted by the experience.

I wasn't bothered that there were other kids there. I wasn't bothered by anything. I was completely hooked. I already knew how to read. After that day, I asked my mom to take me to the library every day. I started school two months later and I was overjoyed to learn the school also had a library. And when it came time for college, there was only one major that interested me. Library sciences.

"I love books," I say because it's not a lie.

He gives me a look that says he doesn't believe me.

"What? Don't you like libraries? You must, based on the one you have here." I pause. "Have you ever even been to the library in town?"

His jaw clenches, and he looks down for a moment and then back at me. "Yes."

I'm surprised by his answer. Why would he have been there?

"You have?" I ask.

He nods. "That's a story for another day."

I look back at the screen and watch for a few minutes.

"Can you tell the story now?" I finally ask, giving up on paying attention to the film.

We turn to face each other.

"My mom loved going. She used to take me for story time with Mrs. Hatcher."

I can't stop the grin from spreading across my face. "I loved her story times! They were the best."

He returns my smile with one of his own, his blue eyes dancing. "You went too?"

I nod excitedly. "That's how I first fell in love with books."

I'm quiet for a beat. There's a question I've had since the first night here and I haven't been brave enough to ask it, but Adam seems different today.

"Can I ask you a question?"

He nods.

"Why can't I go to the west wing?"

His jaw tightens again. "That's my private quarters and..." He trails off.

"Your parents' private quarters?" I ask softly.

He nods. I want to ask a million questions about them, but I feel like I'm already treading on thin ice. As if one more question might push him over the edge.

"You want to see it?" he asks, and my jaw falls open in shock.

"Uh, heck yeah!" I reply.

He chuckles and pulls out a remote from his pocket, hitting pause on the film. Down here with no windows in sight, I've lost track of time. It can't be too late since we're only three hours into a movie marathon. Maybe lunchtime?

I follow Adam back through the maze and up the grand staircase and then we turn left. At first, this wing seems like the other, just more corridors. When we reach the end of the main corridor, there are two large wooden doors. Not as large or fancy as the library, but not small by any means.

Adam takes a breath and opens the door. My eyes widen as I take in the room. I don't know what I expected to see, but certainly not this.

CHAPTER NINE

Adam

I watch her face morph into surprise. My mother had a thing for roses and she had so many in the garden that my father had an atrium made as part of their bedroom. When you enter what was just a standard sitting area before you get to the bedroom, you are now entering a greenhouse designed for roses. There are easily a dozen varieties of them here. The smell is usually what hits you first.

And fuck did that smell mess with me for years. At first, I had made Mrs. Potter tend to them because I couldn't bear it. But now, it's the opposite. It makes me feel close to my mother.

"How? I...there's so many," Isa stammers as she takes a step and stops, clearly waiting for my approval. I nod and motion for her to enter the room.

She takes more steps, tentative steps. I follow her, pressing a hand to her lower back, urging her forward. Once inside, she breathes in deeply.

"The smell..." She trails off as a smile spreads across her face.

"My mother loved roses. After...well, I couldn't bear to have them die. Mrs. Potter used to care for them, but now, I do. I've automated most of it, but once a week, I come in here and trim and cut some bouquets. It makes me feel...well, it reminds me of her, and where that once was very hard for me, it now is a comfort," I admit out loud for maybe the first time. How is this woman in just a matter of days unraveling everything I've kept bundled up for so long?

I watch Isa lean down and gently take a rose in her hand as she smells it. Her eyelids fall closed as she savors the scent. Fuck, she has no idea how beautiful she looks right now. When she finally finishes, she leans up and presses a kiss to my lips.

I don't move at the shock of her boldness.

"Thank you for sharing this with me, Adam," she says softly as she pulls away, but I quickly wrap my arms around her, pressing her against me.

"I don't believe in magic, but I swear you've put some spell on me since you arrived," I murmur as I stare into her dark eyes.

"What's happening between us?" she breathes, her eyes wide. "I...this isn't like me...hell, I haven't even dated in..." She trails off as she blushes.

I place a finger under her chin, prompting her to look up at me.

"I don't know what's happening and I can't promise to be the right man for you. I'm...damaged, Isa. And I don't think there's fixing what's been done. All I know is for the first time in a very long time, I feel things and that's all because of you," I admit, showing my weakness. I never show weakness, but this woman has me doing all kinds of things I don't normally do.

She swallows. "You are not damaged. Maybe a little rough around the edges, but there's hope for you," she says, shyly smiling.

"Come on, there's one more space I want to show you," I say as I step back and take her hand in mine. She follows me back out of my parents' room and down the hall into a smaller corridor.

"Why didn't you want me over here?" she asks.

I turn when we get to my bedroom door. "Because showing you that means..." I trail off because I hate showing kinks in my armor.

"Means, I'd know your heart isn't made of steel?" she asks with a raised eyebrow.

I shrug sheepishly. "Basically. Only a few people know the true me, Isa. I...it was hard enough showing that before, but now...so much rides on me being...in control," I try to explain.

She nods her understanding. "For the record, I'm glad you shared that with me."

I lean down and kiss the tip of her nose. "For the record, I'm glad I shared it with you."

She grins as I open my door. My entry looks fairly normal, but then she turns the corner and stops. I know she sees it.

I step up behind her and look, trying to take it in through her eyes.

My bedroom is circular. It takes up the main turret. There are a few small windows, a small balcony, and a staircase along the side that goes up to another level. One I'm not ready to share with her, maybe ever.

And what does she do...takes off right for it.

"What's up here?" she asks as she starts up the stairs to the small wooden door at the top.

"Nothing, just some old paintings and such," I say much too quickly.

She eyes me suspiciously but steps back down. I unclench

my jaw and watch as she takes in my room. The four-poster bed. The dressers with brass handles. A large closet and bathroom are off to the right. An old tapestry of a manor house in England hangs above the entryway.

"It's very...masculine," she finally declares as she plops on my bed and looks around, and then gets back up. I watch as she steps into the small alcove with doors to the closet, bathroom, and a smaller closet.

"What's in here?" she asks as she opens the door. I know the exact second her eyes adjust to the dim light.

"Oh...I...sorry," she stammers and quickly shuts the door. She's looking everywhere but at me and I want to laugh, but I also don't want to make her any more uncomfortable.

"I...sometimes enjoy trying out new things in the bedroom," I state because it's true and I'm not ashamed of it.

I walk up behind her and open the door again, looking in on some toys I haven't seen or used in a very, very long time.

"Is that...stuff what you like to do?" she stammers.

I press a hand on her shoulder, and she stiffens. Fuck, now I've scared my shy little librarian.

I run my hand down her arm and take her hand. She turns to face me.

"I haven't used any of those things in a long time. I went through a phase after the accident and I thought that was the best way to be...intimate with someone, but I would only use that stuff if someone wanted to use it," I explain.

"So, you aren't some *Fifty Shades of Grey* billionaire that I should be weary of?" she asks with a raised eyebrow.

"Isa, it's a few sex toys in one section of one closet. I hardly have a red room," I reply with a pointed look.

She motions to the closet. "I don't have any...almost any of that stuff. I don't think most people do."

Pink creeps up her neck and I fight my smile. "Almost any of that stuff?" I ask.

She goes from pink to red. "I have...I mean most women have...you know."

I raise my eyebrows, feigning ignorance. "Have what?"

She rolls her eyes and gives my chest a little shove. "You know what."

I raise my hands in a look of confusion. "No, I think you should explain it to me."

She glares at me and something about that look fires me up. Do I secretly yearn for witty banter and a completely infuriating woman? Maybe, I do. Because my dick is already responding to Little Miss Sassy here and I want all of her attitude.

"I have a vibrator...or two, alright. Whatever," she says as she tries to get past me.

I block her and she huffs, crossing her arms in defiance. Fuck, yes. That's what I want, my little siren.

"You have more than one?" I ask.

"Oh my God! Yes! OK! I have three," she says with exacerbation.

I smirk. "Three. Which one is your favorite?"

If fire could shoot from her eyes, it would be happening right now.

"Are you trying to embarrass me, or do you inquire of all your guests on their sex toy preferences?" she asks. That wicked tongue of hers darts out and licks her bottom lip.

"Nope, just yours," I counter as I step squarely in the middle of the entryway into my room.

"The big one with rabbit ears," she answers raising an eyebrow as if to say, "Your move."

I reach into my closet and grab a plastic package just inside the door, glad that I left it right there in easy reach. Who knew it would ever come in handy?

I pull it out and her eyes widen.

"Like this one?" I ask.

She nods and bites her bottom lip.

"What do you like about it?" I ask as I hold it in front of her face.

She looks up at me. Suddenly, her cheeks seem less red. I'm about to ask another question when she takes it from me, opens the plastic, and holds it up to my face.

"Would you like to see what I like about it?" she asks, fighting a smirk.

Oh, Ms. Garren, you have no idea how much I'd love to see that.

I step to the side, and just as I think she's heading to my bed, she drops the vibrator on it and starts toward my entryway.

"Thanks for the tour," she calls out. But I'm faster and have much longer legs. I manage to get to her before she leaves my room. I pin her against my door, my front to her back.

"Let me go," she says against my door.

"I will let you go, but first I need to know that you don't feel the attraction that I feel, that you don't want...more between us. If you don't, then I won't bother you for the rest of your stay here," I assure her.

"And if I do feel that?" she asks.

I swallow hard. "Then, I'm going to pick you up and toss you on my bed and you're going to show me exactly how you like to use that vibrator and then I'm going see how well I can emulate that with my own body," I explain.

"That's very forward of you," she replies.

"I want what I want, Isa. And right now, I want you. I've wanted you for the last two days," I say. "And I'm not a patient man, my beauty. But I would wait, for you I would, if you don't want me like that."

She slowly turns and looks up at me. "I...haven't been with a guy in a long time. And I don't know shit about half those toys you have in there. I...maybe we aren't compatible like that, you know?" she explains.

I smile down at her. "I think we are a lot more compatible than either one of us wants to admit," I state.

She runs her hand down my chest to my cock and grips it through the fabric of my pants. I groan at her bold move.

"Maybe..." she muses.

"You're killing me, beautiful," I grit out from behind clenched teeth.

She smirks a little and I love her cockiness. "If I say yes, then only that vibrator. No other toys from your little closet."

I make an "x" on my chest. "I promise."

"And if I say no to something, it means no," she reiterates.

I take her face in my hands and caress her cheeks with my thumbs. "I will never hurt you like that, Isa. I'm a monster, but even I have my limits. I'd never..." I trail off, hurt that she'd even think that.

It's her little hand on my cheek that has me looking back into her eyes.

"I didn't think you would hurt me, Adam. I just...don't think I'm a sex toy person...beyond some basic stuff," she explains.

I let out a breath. "You are quite the negotiator."

She shrugs. "Only in the bedroom."

Her answer has me laughing. I reach behind her and lift her ass. She wraps her legs around my waist, pressing her core to my erection. I groan and she whimpers.

I place my forehead against hers. "This is going to be fun," I say with a devilish grin.

She laughs and I suddenly feel like I could easily take down James Titan or any other adversary. God, I can't stop thinking about how this woman has weaseled her way into my soul in less than forty-eight hours.

I carry her back to my bed and slowly let her slide down my front.

I step back and look at her. Even in workout clothes, she looks more beautiful.

"You're gorgeous, Isa," I whisper as I begin to take off my clothes, unbuttoning my shirt.

She blushes and shrugs. "You're not so bad yourself," she says, and I might as well have been told I'm the top male model in the country. "Geez, calm down over there, peacock."

I laugh. "I admit, I sort of want to do this with your librarian clothes on."

She rolls her eyes. "It's always the librarian thing," she mutters as she whips off her t-shirt.

I shrug. "Is that bad?" She rolls down her leggings and pulls them off along with her socks and shoes.

"It's a fetish," she answers.

She's standing in front of me in a sports bra and underwear and nothing else. I pull off my pants, socks, and shoes and step toward her after tossing my shirt to the side.

"I think my fetish is just...Isa," I whisper against her jaw as I place a kiss there.

She shivers. "That's an unusual fetish," she murmurs.

"It is...but I can't seem to get enough of her."

She lets out a nervous laugh. "You sure about that?"

I pull back and cup her jaw in my hand, running my thumb over her bottom lip. "I've never been more sure of anything in my entire life."

She reaches down and pulls up her bra, dropping it beside her. I look down and I swear her breasts are even better than when I saw them for half a second nearly two days ago.

I take my free hand and cup one. The perfect handful. I gently run a finger over her nipple, and she lets out a long breath.

"You have perfect breasts, Isa," I say before I take my

hands and lift her onto my bed. My bed's height is very specific, and right now, I'm more thankful for that than ever.

I hook my thumbs in her panties and pull them down her legs. Then very slowly, I place one of her feet on the wooden beam just below the mattress and then the other one. It provides her good support while still allowing me access to all of her.

I glance down at her bare pussy.

She blushes. "I...Elisha and I had a spa day last week. It was my birthday and...anyhow, that was included."

I smile as I run my finger along her folds. "I approve, but I'd approve no matter how you chose to maintain this part of you. As long as it was mine, that's all that would matter."

I reach for the vibrator on the bed. "Show me how you use it, Isa. Teach me what you like."

"Holy shitballs! You have no idea how much of a book boyfriend you sound like right now, do you?" she says as she takes the vibrator.

"I don't know what that is, but if it's a man who wants to please a woman, then I guess that's me. Show me," I encourage as I place my hand over hers, and together, we bring the vibrator between her legs.

CHAPTER TEN

Isa

He flips the vibrator on with a flick of his thumb and I press it against me. My head falls back onto the bed.

"Show me," he says one last time, his voice gruff as if it's taking all his restraint to ask me.

I begin to move it, getting it slick with my need and pressing it slowly inside me and then back out to my clit. I repeat this over and over before sliding it all the way inside.

When I'm nearly there, he rips the vibrator from my hand and tosses it aside.

"I was—" I start to protest until his lips seal over my clit and I cry out from the suction and the flicking of his tongue. Holy fuck! This man is a sex god!

He doesn't let up as he moves his fingers inside me. Stretching me wide with scissor-like movements. My thighs press against his head, but he doesn't seem to care, nor does he flinch as I grip his hair. His beard is rough against my tender flesh but something about that drives me wild, just like with our kiss.

"Don't stop...so close," I murmur as I feel my release build again. He doubles his efforts, adding a third finger and curling them inside me. When he sucks harder on my clit, I feel myself free-fall. My entire body trembles and then releases all at once. Some strange strangled noise is emitted from the back of my throat but I'm only half-aware as my body becomes like gelatin on the mattress.

Adam's head moves up my abdomen and he takes his time licking and sucking on my nipples. His face and beard are wet from me and something about that is hot as fuck. Elisha is never going to believe this. Hell, I barely believe it and it's happening right now.

"I have one toy that I think you might like, based on your vibrator preference," Adam says against my right breast.

"Uh, maybe?" I respond as I start to come back to life.

He leaves me for a moment and goes to the closet. He returns holding some sort of thing that based on the shape, I'm guessing goes around his dick and it's got little rabbit ears protruding...oh. He drops his boxer briefs, and my eyes widen. Holy shit, this man is well-endowed.

He reaches into his side drawer and pulls out condoms. I watch him roll one on and place the device at the base of his cock. He turns it on and groans.

I reach out and he wraps both our hands around his dick. "You like this idea?" he asks, his voice gravelly.

"I think I do," I agree hesitantly.

"Good, 'cause I'm liking it," he agrees as he leans over me and together we guide his cock up and down over my wet flesh until the crown catches on my entrance.

He looks at me as if seeking approval one last time. I flex my hips up taking him inside me just an inch. And that's all the incentive he needs as he thrusts inside me, those little rabbit ears hitting my clit.

"Oh my God!" I cry out as I grip his shoulders. He slams in and out of me, the vibrating ears teasing me with each thrust. The sensations are almost too much but I also want more.

He takes my legs and brings them up to his shoulders and leans down, exposing me at just the right angle for him to slide barely out and back in so those little vibrating ears don't leave my clit.

"Don't stop, Adam, please don't stop," I beg, my voice barely recognizable. I don't think I've ever been so desperate to come in my entire life.

His thrusts become deeper and harder, his cock barely leaving me. I feel the need build deep inside.

"I can't last much longer, Isa. It's too much...come with me," he pleads, and just like that he slams deep one last time and I nearly lose consciousness. My whole body tenses up as I fall over the edge. I realize he's coming at some point, my name is grunted from his lips but I'm so relaxed that I can't even open my eyelids to watch him. His cock jerks inside me with little spasms and then he carefully pulls out and rolls to the side.

"Did I say sex toys were strange? Because I was wrong. That was...fucking awesome," I admit with my eyelids still closed.

His laughter fills the silence and I feel him lean over me and press a kiss to my lips. "Glad I could change your mind. They are all about pleasure and that's all I want to bring you, my beauty. Complete and utter pleasure."

I open my eyelids and look up at him. "When can you bring me complete and utter pleasure again? Because I'm ready when you are," I declare.

He grins down at me. "Well, you're in luck because of

extenuating circumstances, my schedule is one hundred percent free and clear for the rest of the day."

"I guess it's my lucky day," I reply as I roll over. I hear a phone buzz from somewhere in the room.

I start to get up to look for it but Adam pins me down. "They can wait," he growls as he kisses along my throat.

"What if it's important?" I ask.

He looks at me. "Nothing but this"—he motions between us—"is important at this moment. Whatever it is, can wait."

The phone buzzes again.

"I guess the cell phone tower must be working," I state. I start to get up to find mine but I'm suddenly airborne and over Adam's shoulder.

"Adam!" I screech with a laugh. He slaps my ass and...do I find that hot? Yes, why, yes I do. My brows are still furrowed in confusion over my newfound kink when he sets me on the counter in his bathroom. I glance over to see the largest, most beautiful indoor hot tub. He begins reaching for the shower door handle.

"We are going to—"

"Take a bubble bath in that?" I squeak as I point excitedly at the tub.

He turns and looks at it as though he's never even realized he had a tub there. Then, he turns to me. "You want to..." He trails off as he glances back at the tub.

"Please!" I whine, which is very unlike me, but I haven't had a nice bubble bath in years. My parents ripped out their bathtub and put in a shower and I only have a shower in my little apartment.

"Really?" he asks, scratching the back of his head as if I've just asked if we can frolic naked down Main Street.

I grin and nod vigorously. "Please!"

He shrugs and pushes a lever that pulls the drain cover

down and then turns on the water. "I...uh, how warm do you want it?" he asks.

I crane my neck and see there's an actual dial with temperatures on it. "Uh, I have no idea. Really warm?"

He chuckles. "I have no idea what *really warm* means, but let's try this," he suggests as he picks a temperature.

"Bubbles?" I ask with a hopeful glance toward what looks like some type of soap container on the ledge behind the tub.

He frowns and reaches over to examine it. "I don't even think I've ever noticed this before," he muses as he pours a little into the tub.

"I'd be careful with the—"

A large amount falls in and I grimace.

"Amount," I finish as the bubbles start multiplying.

"Oh, fuck," he says as he starts scooping up bubbles and tossing them in the shower.

I giggle. "I think that was too much soap."

"You think?" he asks as he continues attempting in vain to get the bubble situation under control.

I jump down and reach over him, turning the faucet off. The bubbles cease multiplying, and Adam looks over at me.

"Why didn't I think of that?" he grumbles.

"Lack of experience?" I ask.

"How did you think of it?" he asks.

I shrug and tap the side of my head. "High IQ."

Adam glares at me and then promptly picks me up and gets into the tub, lowering us into a cloud of bubbles.

I laugh as he arranges me between his legs and reaches for a sponge that's in a basket on the shelf behind us.

"You seriously have never used this tub?" I ask as he begins to pour some soap on the sponge.

"Nope."

"Not even with other women?" I question.

He tenses. "I've only had a few women here and it was

more for a quick fuck. They didn't exactly stick around for tubby time."

A laugh escapes me. "Tubby time?"

"Isn't that what it's called?" he questions as he begins to rub the sponge over my chest.

I crane my neck to look up at him. "Yeah, if we were like two years old."

"Oh," he says, his brows furrowing as he continues to rub the sponge over my skin.

"Do you want the jets on?" he asks after a moment.

"Say less," I tease.

"Sooo...yes?"

I laugh. "Yes, please." He presses a button and jets start pumping water against us. It's delightful.

"When was the last time you had a guest here?" I inquire as I close my eyes and enjoy the jets massaging my legs.

"Uh...hmmm...I had two men come here a few months ago for a business meeting."

"A few months ago?" I shriek. I swivel in the water and his hands come under my legs, helping me to place a knee on either side of him. "Adam! Do you ever see people?"

He glares at me. "Yes."

"When?"

"I take the helicopter a few times a month to the city and meet with the board. And I typically have a few business meetings while I'm there."

"And?"

"And...like I said, once in a while, I meet up with a few women that I've hung out with socially in the past. But I've been busy lately. This asshole wants to buy my company and I'm not selling it."

"Oh. It sounds serious," I say with a frown. I hadn't given his actual day-to-day business operations any thought.

I feel his whole body tense as he speaks and I don't like

that he's anxious. I begin to massage his shoulders and I feel his muscles relax. His hands settle on my hips. His dick seems to come to life again and it hardens against my belly.

I look down and I swear he seems larger than before. Is that even possible? Maybe the water is magnifying him? Or the last few days have left me completely devoid of normal senses? Well, I can't argue with myself about that last point.

I move my hips and settle over his erection, and he groans.

"What if I told you that I'm on the pill?" I offer because for some reason, I don't want any barriers between us. My logical brain tells me this is a bad idea, and that I should be more careful. Can I trust him?

His hands still, tightening on my thighs. "I don't have sex without condoms," he states.

"Oh," I answer, suddenly feeling silly. Why would I even suggest that? We just met. God, I'm so stupid.

His right hand leaves my hip and comes up to stroke my face. "It's not like that...I...have some trust issues," he admits.

My eyes widen. "Care to expand on that, Mr. Wellington?"

His stare seems to intensify at my use of his formal name. Either Adam has a "yes, sir" kink or he's been groomed to turn into a robot alphahole CEO when I use it.

"Another time," he offers, and I swear I see a flash of hurt on his face. Did someone break his heart? No. No, that's not possible. Not Adam Wellington. The fact that he's lowered his walls this far has to be some snowstorm miracle.

"OK," I reply slowly as I weigh his words.

"Wait here," he says softly as he lifts me and sets me on the other side of the tub. He grabs a towel and walks out of the room, returning a moment later and dropping the towel. He's already got a condom on. He turns on the shower and presses a button and steam begins to fill the room.

"You have a hot tub and a steam shower in here?" I ask.

Shrugging, he holds out a hand and helps me out of the tub. I'm completely covered in bubbles as if I'm wearing some sort of bubble bikini.

He pulls me into the shower, or at least I think it's the shower, because there's so much steam. I hear the shower door shut and then he's pressing me against a heated wall of tiles. His lips trail wet kisses along my jawline.

"Forget the red room, I think the shower room is much better," I whimper.

He takes my chin in his hand, and I look into his eyes. His hair is wet from the steam, and he looks absolutely carnal. "What are you doing to me?" he growls, but before I can contemplate an answer or tell him I feel the same, his lips crash to mine. This kiss is possessive. His lips and tongue own my mouth. I barely register his hands reaching down and grabbing my ass, dragging me up his body. I hardly have time to wrap my legs around his waist when he slams his erection into me. The breath leaves my lungs at the sudden invasion. And then he rolls his hips and slides all the way out and back inside, pinning me to the wall. I'm a ragdoll, caught between the tiles and this beast of a man. It's almost like he's using me like he's trying to fuck the feelings he might have away.

"Adam," I soothe as I run a hand that was gripping his shoulder, over his back.

His eyes fly open, and he stops moving, his erection pulses inside me. "Fuck," he grunts. His right hand releases my ass and comes up to caress my cheek. "I'm sorry, beautiful. I...got carried away."

I swallow at his sudden change to a gentle giant. I nod and he places a gentle kiss on my lips.

"Are you OK? Did I hurt you?" he manages from behind gritted teeth.

I shake my head and swallow. "I'm alright. That was just... intense," I add. "But...I didn't *not* like it."

He smiles against my jaw. "We should find out what else you don't *not* like."

"Game on, pretty boy," I whisper.

He looks back into my eyes. "Where the hell have you been hiding?"

I shrug. "The library. You should stop by more often."

He chuckles as he begins to move again. This time slower, letting me feel every inch of him. We build the pace with each punishing thrust, finding our rhythm. I rub myself against him, seeking as much friction as possible. He reaches between us while still keeping me pinned to the wall. He finds my sensitive nub and rubs it in tiny circles. I feel my frenzy building.

"Adam," I whimper in desperation.

"I'm coming, beauty, I'm coming," he grunts out as we both fall over the edge.

When we come back down to reality and our breathing slows, he helps me to stand and then washes us before leading me back to bed.

"What time is it?" I ask.

He grabs his phone. "Four," he answers.

"We've been up here all afternoon?" I say way too loudly.

"Yep," he answers as if four-hour sex sessions are no big deal. I think my combined last two boyfriends only lasted four minutes between them. I am most definitely going to be sore tomorrow.

I watch as he continues looking at his phone. "Do you have cell reception?" I ask.

He nods.

I scurry off the bed and grab my phone. Forty-five missed text messages.

I roll my eyes.

There are a few from my parents. So, I text them back

that I'm fine and still stuck out at the Wellington Estate with Felipe. I have separate texts from Bastian and Elisha.

Bastian: Are you surviving with Mr. Personality?

Bastian: Please tell me you didn't murder him. He's big and the ground is frozen.

Bastian: Did he murder you?

Bastian: WHY IS NO ONE RESPONDING?

I roll my eyes again and then read Elisha's text messages.

Elisha: So? How's it going? Did we get those books?

I frown. I haven't even thought about the books since yesterday when he showed them to me.

Elisha: You're boring and so I stalked Adam Wellington online. HOLY SHITBALLS! I don't know what he looks like now, but like ten years ago…(flames emoji).

Elisha: Gurlll…if you don't try to get a piece of that while you're stuck out there, then I'm going to find my old cross-country skis and come over.

My eyes widen when I see the next text. It's a group chat with Bastian, Max, and Elisha.

Bastian: Elisha, have you heard from Isa?

Max: I heard from Joe who spoke to Harry who's married to Kelly whose dad works for the telecom company that the cell tower by the estate is out.

Elisha: Say what?

Bastian: Translation: Max sucks at texting. The cell tower is down, so maybe that's why we can't get ahold of Adam or Isa?

Elisha: Oh. Right.

Bastian: But Adam isn't picking up the landline or answering emails. I hope the power didn't go out or worse, the Wi-Fi!

Elisha: Calm down there, Mr. Final Destination. There are worse things than no Wi-Fi.

Bastian: Like what?

Elisha: (eye-rolling emoji)

Bastian: Seriously, what could be worse?

Max: Ignore Bastian, he's...just ignore him.

Bastian: I used to like you.

Max: You didn't have a problem earlier today. (winking emoji)

Elisha: Ewww. This is an intimate-relationship-free zone.

Max: Oh come on...we all know you secretly want a piece of Mason Conover.

Elisha: Uh, no.

Bastian: How much did your nose grow just now?

Elisha: Whatever. Mason's fine, but we're just friends.

Max: Friends. Is that what the kids are calling it now?

Elisha: (eye-rolling emoji)

Bastian: I am worried about them. Adam is...Adam. And Isa went in there with some massive lady balls, which means there are two alphas stuck in that house right now...that defies the law of nature.

Max: Shit. Adam didn't know she was coming over, right?

Bastian: Nope.

Elisha: Should I send out a search party? It's been two days and I still haven't heard from her.

Bastian: If we don't hear anything by tomorrow, I'm getting out my old snowshoes.

Max: Le sigh. You're not going alone. Get mine out too.

Elisha: Best of luck. I'm staying right here by my fireplace.

Bastian: If you don't hear from us by tomorrow, send that search party.

Elisha: Noted.

I look over at Adam, who's furiously typing away.

"I think the cell tower is most definitely working again," I say as I type a response to the group chat.

Me: We are alive. No murders...yet. Hopefully, they can get the roads plowed tomorrow once this storm clears. We lost power but the backup generator is now working and the cable lines got pulled up by a tree. So no Wi-Fi or landlines.

Felipe, who has settled by the foot of the bed, whines.

"I think the dogs need dinner and a bathroom break," Adam says as he stands and throws on a robe. He offers me a button-down shirt and boxer shorts.

"Chill, Felipe. We're going to feed you," I say to my dog as Adam and I head toward the kitchen.

The dogs jostle for the head-of-the-pack position as we meander through corridors. Felipe bumps into a side table and knocks a vase off it. The vase crashes to the floor and I freeze like a deer in the headlights.

"Oh, God! Please tell me that's a reproduction and not some priceless artifact," I yelp as I lunge for my dog and tell him to sit.

All three dogs respond to my command and sit along the hallway.

Adam looks down at it and shrugs. "It's a five-hundred-year-old Ming dynasty vase worth several millions," he states.

I hear his words but then everything gets a little fuzzy as if he's in a tunnel. My vision starts to look like an old television screen with no reception. And then everything goes black.

CHAPTER ELEVEN

Adam

Thank God I was close enough to catch her. Fine, it was a little mean to lie, but I was just joking. It's a simple reproduction. Our Ming vases are carefully stored in the dining room cabinets.

The dogs are crowded around us, and Felipe is licking Isa's face.

"Isa, beautiful, wake up," I say softly as I touch her cheek while cradling her body with my other arm.

She stirs and opens her big, brown eyes. "I...I can't afford..." She trails off.

"I was joking. It's not real. I'm sorry...I didn't think you'd believe me," I try to explain but feel more and more like a jackass with every word I utter.

She frowns. "It's not real?"

I shake my head.

She glares at me. "Fuck you! That's not remotely funny,"

she hisses as she climbs out of my arms and stands, swaying slightly. I grab her arm.

"I'm sorry," I reiterate a little more aggravated. "Let's get you food, too."

I help her down to the kitchen, linking my arm with hers. She doesn't say a word to me, which means she's probably pissed.

Great.

I motion for her to sit on a stool, and I let the dogs out and feed them. Then, I look around the freezer and find some containers of Mrs. Potter's famous loaded potato soup. She's still known to cook me my favorite meals even with Bastian around. I warm it in a pot on the stove and pour it into two large bowls, placing one in front of Isa and another next to her where I take a seat on the second stool. We eat in silence. Isa stands to clear our bowls when we finish, but I take hers and start doing it myself.

"I can do it," she insists, starting to jump off the stool. I'm in front of her in an instant, wedging myself between her legs.

"I. Am. Sorry," I bite out through clenched teeth. "I shouldn't have teased about that. I...sometimes forget not everyone has...I'm an idiot," I stammer through my apology. And I mean it. I saw Isa's car if you can call it that. Her clothes look like they are hanging on by a thread. She doesn't have the type of money that I have. I should do better in understanding this. I need to do better.

She rolls her eyes. "Now, that we can agree on."

I give her a pointed look and she gives me one right back. Damn, this woman! Even when she's driving me crazy, I find her irresistible.

I lean in and cup her face with my hands. "You drive me crazy," I growl.

"Right back at you, Mr. Wellington," she replies.

I press my lips to hers and enjoy the little whimpers she

makes as I show her just how crazy she drives me. I'm lost in her, in us, when a voice from behind me has me quickly turning and putting my arms out to protect Isa.

"Well, I didn't have this on my winter storm bingo card," Bastian says with a smirk as he leans against the hallway doorjamb.

"Christ! You scared the shit out of me," I grumble.

Isa leans her head on my shoulder. "Hi, Bastian."

He raises an eyebrow. "Hi, Isa. Nice outfit."

I place a protective hand on her knee and then quickly release it. Bastian is with Max. I shouldn't feel so possessive over Isa, let alone in front of Bastian.

I need to play this off as a snowstorm fling. If Bastian thinks I'm serious, all the staff will be up in my grill, and I can't have that. I shudder as I remember how they all doted on me after my parents died. The Potters, Bastian, even Ben, the gardener, and my assistant, Cruz, who had just started at the company. I don't want that again. I prefer to operate in the shadows, being left to get my work done and only having to be public when I go to the city for business.

I step away from Isa. "I'm going to work out. Did they clear the roads already?" I ask, peering out the one small window in the kitchen. I frown. It's stopped snowing, but there's definitely no way that Bastian drove here.

"Un, nope. I have snowshoes, and when the storm stopped, I figured I'd hike over here for my workout and make sure you two kids hadn't killed each other," he says with a smirk.

I glare at him which only has him widening his devious smile. Clearly, I need to be more convincing that I don't give a shit about Isa.

"Are you staying?" I ask as I head to the door on the opposite side of the room.

"Since you only ate some soup, I'll make you all dinner for

later, but then I should head back. Sun's going down and Max will murder me if I'm out past bedtime. He tried to come with me, but that would have doubled the time it took to get here," he replies with a wink at Isa.

Isa giggles. "I can help...just let me change," she says.

"Don't get dressed up on my account," Bastian teases as I swing the door open and head to my room to put on gym clothes.

I pass Isa and Bastian on the way back to the gym. She smiles at me, and I nod in her direction. "I'll see you down at dinner. I need to work out and send a few work emails," I state as I work to keep my hands from touching her skin. It takes all my willpower to pass her without throwing her up against the wall and kissing the ever-loving hell out of her again.

"Oh, OK," she manages as she stops. I can feel her eyes on me as I make my way to the east wing.

I get on my treadmill and run until my legs begin to shake. I stop the device and lean on the control board. I need to get a grip. I've known this woman for three days. I can't let her get under my armor. I won't do that again...at least not until I know I can one hundred percent trust her, which may be never.

I take my time showering. A ding on the intercom system tells me dinner is ready.

I make my way downstairs and find Isa leaning against the dining room table chatting away with Bastian. She's still in my clothes and something about that makes me immensely pleased.

"Thank you, Bastian. You didn't have to cook diner and stay. Your next paycheck will reflect my gratitude for coming out here in a snowstorm," I say as I take my seat.

He rolls his eyes and grins at Isa. "I mean...if you want to, but I didn't hike out here for some kind of bonus, you jackass. OK, kids." I glare at him, and he clears his throat, trying to return to his normal professional self, which is nearly impossible apparently.

"Tonight, we have a lobster bisque, followed by a rack of lamb and roasted asparagus. Isa has graciously assisted me in baking a pumpkin pie for dessert. If it's alright with you, Mr. Wellington," he says, emphasizing my name and my glare intensifies, "I will take my leave. I can stop back by tomorrow, likely midday unless the plows can get out here." He pauses. "Uh, I'm letting you know that they are super not likely to get out here because that's a shit ton of snow and it's going to take a good day or two to plow the main roads."

I crack my neck. Bastian is typically informal around me, but he never acts like this on the rare occasion we've had guests in the house.

"Anyhoo," he says, the word coming out thick with his waning French accent. He's managed to perfect his English but every once in a while, I hear that French come out.

"OK, I'll see you tomorrow. Text me if you need something. Oh, and I called about the power. The power company has started trying to restore it to the area. They seem to think you should have power by tonight or tomorrow," he adds. "I'm going to check on the Potters before I head home."

I nod. "Thank you, Bastian. Please be safe. And tell Mrs. Potter to text me if she needs anything," I add as I watch him leave the room. He only lives about three miles away as the crow flies. Many days, he runs here on a trail that ends by a park near his cul-de-sac on the edge of town. I shouldn't be so annoyed. He's gone above and beyond today. He's a good employee and an even better friend. I'll make sure he gets a huge bonus this month.

The room seems extra silent when Bastian exits. His presence is as loud as his voice.

I glance over at Isa as I try the soup. It's excellent, which is nothing less than I expect from Bastian's cooking.

"That was nice of Bastian to come here," Isa says, breaking the silence.

"Yes. He's a good man," I reply. The silence between us feels awkward, unlike the comfortable silences over the past few days.

"I would snowshoe back with him, but I don't think I'm adequately dressed," she says as she looks down at my over-sized clothes on her petite frame.

"You will do no such thing. Once the roads are clear and safe, you can take that death trap back home. Although, I prefer you not take that car. I can arrange for you to use one of mine until you can acquire something that won't kill you," I state with a raised eyebrow.

She rolls her eyes. "I'll be just fine in my car," she answers before finishing her soup and starting on her lamb and asparagus. "Bastian mentioned the horses? Should I be worried that we haven't been feeding them?" she asks.

"No. They are fine. Mr. Potter left them extra feed. We have an automatic feeder rigged up to give them feed when there's a storm or something," I explain.

"Oh," she says quietly. I realize my tone is a little harsh, even with Bastian gone.

"I'd invite you out to the barn, but..." I look toward where her feet are beneath the table. "I don't think you have the proper shoes."

"Right," she replies quietly as she looks down at her feet.

"Now that we have cell service, I need to do some work tonight," I announce as I stand to clear my dishes.

She's quiet for a beat. "Leave it. I can clear dinner if you have work to do."

Her words are punctuated and seem forced. Is she mad at me because I have to work?

And this is why I don't do relationships. I grimace at the memory of Stephanie. It was my job that had started the arguments. It was my work that had been her excuse for betrayal. I can see how a relationship with Isa would lead right back to that same problem.

I give her a small nod. "Thank you," I manage as I leave and head to my office, hoping my hotspot on my phone is enough to get some work done on my laptop.

I lose track of time, and when I look up from a report, I see that's it's ten o'clock. Shit.

I log out and head out to search for Isa. She's not in the kitchen or my room and neither are the dogs. I find her fast asleep in an armchair in the library, a book lying on her lap, the dogs lying on the floor around her. I study her for a long beat, taking in the way her eyelashes flutter against her cheeks as she dreams, the way her hair that's escaped her bun falls across her face, and the way her glasses have slid down her nose. She doesn't snore, but her loud breathing tells me she's deeply asleep.

I take the book and set it on the side table and then debate what to do. Ultimately, I decide not to disturb her. I find a throw blanket in the cabinet and place it over her. I can't help running my fingers over her cheek.

"Sleep well, my beauty," I whisper. I wish I could keep you. I wish I was the right man for you. I wish I could hear your laugh echoing in the walls of this prison that I've built for myself.

I head up to my room, resigned to the fact that the dogs will not follow me. My sleep is interrupted by nightmares. I wake with a start at eight in the morning. I hear the plow. I guess my guest *will* be leaving today. I get out of bed and shower and then go to find Isa.

I frown when I get to the library. She's not there. I search for her and realize my dogs are lying in the entryway without

Felipe. Looking out front, I don't see her car. What the fuck?

I run up to her room. *Her room.* I don't let myself read too far into that thought. I throw open a door and look inside. The bed is neatly made. All traces of Isa have vanished, as if she had never been here at all.

The only thing that tells me she really existed is a piece of paper lying on the bed.

Mr. Wellington,

Thank you for accommodating me during the storm.

Best Wishes,

Isa

What in the actual fuck? Does she think she can just leave me like that?

I hear the door open, and I race downstairs hoping to find Isa has returned.

"Wow, so much excitement to see me!" Bastian laughs as he shuts the door. He glances back out front. "Plow came early. I know, I know, I'm as shocked as you," he adds as he reaches into his bag and pulls out his phone. He pauses when he looks at my face.

"You alright?" Then he frowns. "Where's Isa?"

I feel anger rise in me. We had a deal. She promised to stay. Did she take the books? "She left."

"Oh…OK, then. I'm going to the kitchen," he says as he scurries away like an injured animal afraid I'll make it worse.

I walk in long strides back into the library and look up at the bookshelf containing my collection of first editions. Untouched. She didn't take them. I furrow my eyebrows in confusion. She didn't take what she came for and she didn't stay. I shouldn't care. I should let her stay away. After all, that's what I was trying to do yesterday. I should close the door on whatever happened the last three days, but something inside me can't. Something inside me still wants her, needs her. I swallow at the realization of what I'm about to do. I'm going to make her see me again, and these books are my collateral.

I hear Mrs. Potter's voice. I press the call button on the intercom.

"Good morning, Mr. Wellington. I just arrived. Ben cleared the path for us this morning. Can I get you something?" she answers, her gentle, soothing voice is like balm on my soul.

I let myself take a deep breath. "Can Mr. Potter ready Apollo? And have Bastian send some carrots down to the stables," I ask.

"Of course, Mr. Wellington," Mrs. Potter replies.

"What? Carrots? What is this Oregon Trail?" Bastian's voice breaks in from the background.

"Thank you, Mrs. Potter. And fuck off, Bastian," I reply.

"Oh, uh, of course, dear," she replies and I hear the swatting of a towel against what I assume is Bastian who curses. Shit. Do I never thank her? I sigh as I head back to my room to get my riding clothes on. Time to go find Ms. Garren.

CHAPTER TWELVE

Isa

"And then, I just left," I finish as I drink my coffee. Elisha leans her elbows against the small bistro tabletop.

"You didn't even say goodbye?" Max asks with raised eyebrows.

I shrug. "Why bother?"

I've left out the whole sex-with-Adam part of this story, but I've shared everything else, including that we kissed.

"Shit. I owe Bastian fifty bucks," he says as he leans back in his chair.

My friend Ella Foster is standing wide-eyed by the door. She's been threatening to leave for work for the past thirty minutes. "Wow. I wish I could stay longer and hear more, but I'm already late. I'll see you all later," she says as she waves goodbye.

Elisha rolls her eyes at Max and looks back at me. "Honey, what about the books?"

I shake my head as I feel tears well in my eyes. "I...I didn't take them."

Elisha squeezes my hand and looks at Max. "We can get Bastian to bring them here?"

Max purses his lips. "Maybe. I can ask...I just...Adam is not going to like that you just left."

I narrow my eyes at Max. Since when is he an expert on Adam Wellington, we've barely ever discussed Adam. "Does it look like I care?"

He shakes his head, pressing his lips together. "Well, I'm going to head over to the restaurant. I need to make sure our new sous chef has all his paperwork filled out." Max stands. "Later, ladies."

We both wave and I look at Elisha. Most of the morning crowd has left, or at least the smaller crowd as some people haven't ventured out yet. I couldn't even find a parking spot since the snow isn't fully plowed yet, but my favorite library patron, a little old man named Mr. Arkin, took pity on me and let me use his extra garage space.

Felipe was less than excited to be home alone when I left, but I need to get to the library and make sure our plumbing didn't freeze.

"You slept with him, didn't you?" Elisha hisses as her eyes dart to the only customers in here besides me, a couple in their mid-thirties who are sitting typing on their laptops while sipping lattes.

"Shhh," I say, using my best librarian voice.

"I fucking knew it!" she whisper-yells.

I glare at her.

"What? Max and Bastian both owe me one hundred dollars!" she says loudly. The couple pauses and looks over at us.

She doesn't even look sheepish.

"Seriously. You're a total ho bag," I grumble.

"Girl, you needed it. How was it? Are the rumors true? Is he hung like his horses? Does he still look as hot as those photos I found online? Tell me he looks like a supermodel!" she squeals, her excitement palpable. If I ever speak to Adam again, I'm going to tell him he needs to start coming into town so everyone here isn't making up absurd rumors about him.

"Calm down there, killer. He—"

Elisha's mouth drops open as her gaze looks past me. I frown and turn. "Holy fuckballs," I whisper. I rub my eyes because the only logical explanation is that I'm hallucinating. Nope. Adam is still riding a horse down the street and coming right toward the café.

"Well, I'll be a princess in a motherfucking real-life fairy tale," Elisha says as she tries to gain her composure.

He really does look like a fairy-tale prince riding on his trusty steed. He's trimmed his beard. A lock of his wavy hair falls over one eye. Stubble dots his cheeks and chin. He's wearing some outfit that screams that he should be on the cover of a high-end outdoors magazine.

I'm in such shock, I don't even know what to say or do. I just sit there, with my mouth gaping as I stare at Adam. He stops his horse right outside the window and hops off. Tying the lead to a light pole, he glances inside the café. I can't look away from him as he pulls open the door and steps inside. His bright blue eyes meet mine and the intensity between us grows like thickening fog with each of his steps.

"Isa," he says in a low gravelly voice that has my lady bits paying close attention.

"Adam," I manage as I attempt to stand, but instead, I knock over the table. Coffee goes spilling everywhere. Elisha quickly grabs a towel as Adam steps around the table and grabs my arm.

"Are you OK?" he asks, his intense gaze searching mine. I pull my arm away so that I can help Elisha wipe up the coffee.

"I'm fine. I...Elisha, let me help," I offer as I lean down just as Adam moves forward and...I smack my head against his crotch. He grunts and my face goes from pink to bloodred.

"Oh my God, are you OK? I'm sorry," I mutter with my face still pinned against his crotch because Elisha has uprighted the table and now we are boxed in against the wall.

I hear the table squeak as Elisha moves it.

"Oops, sorry," she says in a singsongy voice that I know is anything but sorry. I pull my face away from Adam's body and look up. There's a pained expression on his face and I grimace.

"I really am sorry," I whisper.

He just nods and places a hand over himself as if I might headbutt the sensitive area again. He doesn't speak, but he does manage to hold a hand out to help me stand. I accept it and rise to see the chaos I've created. The table toppled over and caused another table and chairs to fall over into a display stand that had coffee on it and now bags of coffee are everywhere, some ripped open, spreading coffee grounds and beans in all directions. The couple in the back is looking at us with wide eyes.

Before I can say anything more, Elisha is standing next to me holding out a broom. "You're lucky that you're my best friend," she says.

I start sweeping up the coffee beans on the floor. "What do you want?" I hiss at Adam. Now, I'm just annoyed. What the hell is he even doing here?

"You didn't take the books," Adam states.

"No shit, Sherlock," I grumble as I dump the beans into a trash can.

"Don't you want them?" he asks.

I continue sweeping because I honestly don't know what to say. Yes, please give me the books? No, take your fucking books and shove them where the sun doesn't shine? I actually started liking you for two seconds but you turned out to be a prick after all? I can't make up my mind.

Adam's hand darts out and grabs the broom, forcing me to pause and look up at him.

"Isa," he starts, his eyes searching mine. God, why does he have to be so ruggedly handsome? Why can't he be hideous? At least when he acts like an asshole, I can hate him, but when he's sincere or kind...fuck. I wish I could bring myself to push my pride aside and say I need the damn books.

But if I admit that, then I admit defeat to Adam and my stubbornness will not allow me to do it. Hell, my stubbornness is how I got into this predicament, to begin with. If only my pride didn't stop me from asking my parents to help with the library.

When I don't reply, Adam clears his throat and suddenly looks all businesslike. What the hell?

"I have a proposition for you," he starts.

Elisha cough-laughs and I glance at her with a harsh glare. She bites her lip and shrugs. Ugh! My friends are so irritating.

"I will still give you the books if you want them, but I want you to go out with me," Adam states as if we are negotiating some sort of business deal.

My eyebrows shoot up to my hairline. "I'm sorry, what?"

"Three dates. You go out with me three times and I will personally hand-deliver the books to the library," he says.

I shove the broom at Elisha and place my hands on my hips. "You said that I could have the books if I stayed the night," I seeth as I raise my right hand and point my finger at his chest. "Or are you just a liar?"

His jaw clenches and he glares back at me. "You left."

"I stayed until it was safe to leave," I state.

"It wasn't safe, not in that death trap you call a car," he replies, motioning outside as if my car is there.

"It got me back home, didn't it?" I reply.

"You broke your promise," he says matter-a-factly. I want to contest his accusation, but it's true, sort of. What did he say? I try to remember his exact words, but it had something to do with the roads being cleared. And they sort of were cleared...sort of.

"No, I didn't. The roads were clear enough for me to go home," I retort, doubling down on my stance.

He groans in frustration and runs his hand over his trimmed beard. "I'm not arguing about this any further. Three dates and you can have the books," he replies.

"And what if I say no?" I raise an eyebrow.

"Then, I guess you're out of luck," he replies. I clench my hands in fists. This man is so exacerbating!

"And what would we do on these *three dates*?" I ask, making air quotes around the last two words.

"I have some work obligations and I need a date for them," he replies.

"So, I'm an escort getting paid in historical books?" I reply in disgust. Who the hell does this man think he is?

"No...no," he says, the first *no* coming out with hostility. "I..." He trails off and looks around us. The couple is still staring at us and so is Elisha.

"Can we speak somewhere...more private?" he asks.

I roll my eyes and grab his hand, hauling him outside. I open the side door and walk up the steps to my apartment. "You coming?" I ask.

He frowns but follows me. I unlock my apartment door and Felipe comes barreling toward me and then past me. He jumps up and places his front paws on Adam's shoulders and licks his face.

Adam laughs. "Good to see you too, Felipe."

"Felipe, down!" I yell.

Felipe whimpers and gets down. He cowers toward his sofa and sits. "Sorry, buddy, it's alright," I say more softly as I walk over and pat his head. His big tail wags and I feel guilty for yelling at him. I glare at Adam because it's all his fault.

"What do you want?" I ask from behind gritted teeth.

Adam looks around us. "Is this...do you live here?" he asks.

I roll my eyes again. "Yes, Captain Obvious. I live here." I look around, realizing it's not exactly the opulence he's used to, and I grimace. I feel my cheeks heat with embarrassment. I normally don't feel bad about where I live because it's all mine. I've worked for everything in here...the threadbare sofa, the secondhand bookcases, the old wing-backed chair that I reupholstered.

Adam walks to my shelves and looks at my books. I don't have many nice things, but I do have a collection of original Nancy Drew novels that I've been collecting for ten years, ever since I found out the ones I read from the 1950s weren't the first editions.

"You collect books," he says quietly.

"I'm a librarian," I state dryly.

He looks back at me. "I..." He trails off again. Suddenly, he looks nervous. He swallows and walks toward me. "May I?" he asks, motioning to the sofa where I've just sat down.

I scoot over and he sits. He smells good...too good. Damn it, Isa! I need to stay strong. Adam Wellington is not the man for me. I look into those blue eyes that I find so mesmerizing. No, he's definitely not...well, mostly not...the man for me.

CHAPTER THIRTEEN

Adam

"You see...I hate women," I start and then clench my jaw. "I mean, not all women. I mean..." I trail off. Idiot! Why am I saying this? I'm an amazing businessman. I can negotiate billion-dollar deals, and here I am stumbling over words.

"I—I'm sorry, what?" Isa stammers, her eyes growing wider with each word I've spoken.

I take a breath and start over. "I need a date for a few upcoming events. You're clearly smart. You're obviously well-read. It would save me a big hassle of finding someone to go with." I pause. "Consider it a business deal. I'll buy you all the dresses you need for the events. I'll pay for everything. You just show up and act charming." I pause again. "You can act charming, right?"

Isa groans and rolls her eyes. "Around everyone but you," she retorts.

I level a stare at her. She glares back at me. I fight the

smile that threatens to emerge. God, this woman is so good at getting under my skin.

"What else?" she asks.

"That's it. Three dates over the next four weeks. And then, I'll bring by the entire collection."

"The entire collection?" she asks.

I nod.

"But I just needed..." She stops herself.

"You may borrow all of them. From the glass cabinet. You remember, right?" I ask.

She nods and I watch her throat constrict as she swallows. "I do," she says quietly.

"Good. Do we have a deal?" I question.

She crosses her arms again and it does nothing to quell my desire for her because it pushes up her breasts in a way that makes me want to lean over and take one in my mouth.

"Eyes up here, Mr. Wellington," Isa scolds.

I grin. "Deal?" I repeat.

She closes her eyes and rubs the bridge of her nose. "I still feel like I'm some sort of escort."

She opens her big brown eyes again and I smirk. "A book escort?" I jest.

She rolls her eyes, but I swear I see a flash of hurt in them and something inside me snaps.

"You are not an escort. This isn't about sex. I...will only do what you want. If you want this all professional, then it's all professional, Isa," I assure her; my voice tense, my jaw clenched. I want to know why she left without a word. I want to know why she didn't take the books. But something inside me tells me not to push her, that if I push her, she'll just run away again. And I don't want that. We only spent a few days together, but she changed me in a matter of hours. I haven't felt this alive in years, and that familiar feeling of having something, something you love, and being afraid of losing it has come rushing back to me. I don't like it, but it's a driving force inside me. If I have to play a game to get her, then I'll play a game. I'm not entirely sure what I'll do if I get her back, but I'll cross that road later. For now, I'm operating in the present. And present me wants Isa by my side.

I go to reach out and touch her, but she pulls back. I feel my jaw tense again. How did we get here? She was writhing under me less than a day ago and now this. What the fuck am I missing? But I continue to rein in what little control I have and decide that I'll keep my distance...for now. Adam, use your fucking negotiation skills.

"Please, Isa. This would really help me out," I say, softening my voice.

Her eyes search mine and her hands clench together in her lap. She closes those big eyes of hers again and then slowly opens them. Fuck. She's so perfect. Part of me still wants to push her away, afraid I'll tarnish her in some way. That my anger gets the best of me and I ruin her.

"Fine," she agrees, her knuckles turning white from her hands clenching so tightly.

I can no longer hold back. I slowly place one of my hands over hers. This time she doesn't pull away. She looks up at me from beneath her lashes and I have to use my self-control again to stop myself from kissing her.

"Just three dinners," I assure her.

"Three dinners," she repeats slowly.

I nod and run my thumb along hers before pulling my hand away.

"The first event is tomorrow night. I'll send Bastian to get you. Be ready at six," I state as I rise and walk out of her pathetic excuse for an apartment.

Her friend is standing outside the café downstairs. She's patting my horse on the side. Apollo seems quite content with her.

"Trying to abduct my stallion?" I ask.

She laughs. "I'm fairly certain he would come willingly."

She pauses and looks over at me. I sigh. She wants to ask questions.

Before I can stop her, she launches into them.

"What do you want with Isa?" she asks point-blank.

I groan. "Nothing. She needs something. I need something. It's a simple business transaction."

"Right," she says, drawing out the last syllable.

"The reasons are between Isa and me. You should ask your friend, not me," I state as I untie Apollo's lead.

Elisha holds out her hand. "I don't think we were properly introduced. I'm Elisha Johnson."

I take her hand and shake it. She grips mine tightly in some kind of warning as she looks me up and down.

"I have a forty-five and a shovel," she states. "Her parents wouldn't hurt a fly, but I would."

I like this woman and I like that Isa has a friend who is willing to stand by her side.

"Noted, Ms. Johnson," I reply. "I sure hope you don't need the shovel."

"And the forty-five?" she asks, raising an eyebrow.

"Well, if you think you need it for protection, far be it from me to deny you that," I state.

She cocks her head to one side. "You're an interesting man, Mr. Wellington. Not at all what I thought you'd be."

"And what was that?" I ask as I mount my horse.

"A complete and total asshole," she states matter-a-factly.

I smirk. "Maybe not a *complete and total* asshole."

She smiles. "Perhaps."

I tip my head toward her and tap my heel against Apollo's side. "Let's go home," I say as my horse takes me back to my estate.

———

Bastian is waiting for me when I come inside. He leans against the wall, crossing his arms and sizing me up. "You sly little fucker," he says in a low voice as a smirk spreads across his face.

"What?" I ask, my voice laced with annoyance. What the fuck is he talking about?

"You seriously are making her go out on three dates to get those books? You don't ever even look at them," he states.

I shrug and head toward my office.

"You really like this woman, don't you?" he asks as he follows behind me.

"None of your business," I growl.

"Fuck. You do. OK. What's the game plan?" he inquires when we reach the double doors.

I turn and look at him. Bastian is tall, nearly as tall as I am. But where I'm broad, he's lean. I'd never hurt him, but right now, I sort of want to throw him into a wall. He's aggravating as fuck.

He senses my annoyance and steps back with his hands up. He gives me a sincere look. "Look, I'm just happy you're interested in someone, and someone good at that. Isa's a good person," he says before turning around. I realize that he has a whole life outside the estate. I mean, I knew he dated Max. But I never thought about all the friends and acquaintances he must have in town. I suppose I've been a selfish prick, too consumed by my own troubles to contemplate my friend's life outside of my world.

He stops a step away from the next corridor and looks at me over his shoulder. "Don't fuck it up."

"You're seriously getting on my last nerve," I declare to my oldest friend. Hell, my only friend.

He grins. "Where are we taking her first?"

"The city. Tomorrow night. The gala," I state.

"The charity gala?" he asks, raising an eyebrow.

"Yes."

"Wow...I mean...OK...that's a big deal," he points out.

"I guess."

He turns back around to face me. His facial features change, so I know he's serious. "Adam...does she know?"

I shake my head. "And don't tell her, you asshat. She doesn't need to know," I snip.

"You should tell her," he suggests.

"What I do or don't tell Isa is none of your concern."

He rolls his eyes. "You are so petulant sometimes. Were you always this grumpy?" he asks, frowning as if trying to remember the past.

"Yes," I declare.

He cracks a lopsided grin. "I suppose you were. But there was a time that you were sort of fun."

"I don't recall," I say dryly.

"I like this for you. Isa is good for you," he says as he turns back around. "Don't fuck it up!" he says again as he leaves me alone in the hallway.

I groan and turn, opening the doors and closing them behind me. I have a date to plan.

CHAPTER FOURTEEN

Isa

Mr. Asshole Wellington: The car is on its way.

I look down at the message on my phone. I grin at the nickname I gave him. It suits him.

I spin in front of my mirror. Adam had a dress, shoes, and jewelry sent over with a hair and makeup specialist this afternoon. The woman, named Gloria, was waiting here when I arrived back from checking on the library. The heat is out again, so I decide to keep it closed until I can get someone out to look at the furnace.

"What do you think, Felipe?" I ask as I take in my appearance.

Felipe groans and rolls over on my bed. I glare at his reflection in the mirror.

"Thanks a lot. I think I look half decent," I say as I smile. I hardly recognize myself. He chose a yellow dress for me. I would never have chosen this color, but it's not an obnoxious yellow and the crystal beading on it is beautiful. There's an ornate rose pattern on it that goes up the skirt. The bodice cinches my waist and the low neckline leaves little to the imagination. I'm not used to looking like this, but I suppose it's appropriate for whatever he has in mind. I'm not aware of any events in town tonight, so I'm curious about where we're going.

A buzz tells me my driver has arrived. I kiss Felipe's head and motion toward his food bowl. "I left you extras, buddy. Be good."

He makes a tired dog noise and rolls over. I laugh and head downstairs. When I open the door, I'm surprised to find Bastian.

"Bastian?" I ask as if he's a mirage.

"Holy shitballs! You look hot as fuck! Adam is going to die," Bastian exclaims as he looks at me. He holds out a hand and spins me in a tight circle.

He lets out a whistle. "Damn. If I batted for the other team, I'd whisk you away now."

I laugh. "You're crazy, you know that?"

He shrugs.

"Why are *you* my driver?" I ask as he opens the door to a town car.

I get inside. He doesn't answer until he's in the driver's seat. "Because I'm the only one Adam trusts with precious cargo. He's not a fan of these," he explains as he pats the steering wheel.

I frown in confusion. "Of steering wheels?"

He laughs but then gives me a serious look in the rearview mirror. "Of cars."

"Oh," I say, still confused. And then it dawns on me, his parents, the accident. "Oh," I say again drawing out the word. That explains the horse.

"Yeah. Since the accident...he's...well, you'll see," he says. I don't quite understand his words. You'll see. See that Adam is a little particular? Yeah, I've already seen that.

"Do you know where we are going tonight?" I ask.

"You'll see," he repeats.

"Bastian," I chide.

He grins at me in the rearview mirror, and I roll my eyes.

"Just enjoy it. When was the last time you went on a date anyhow? The Jurassic period?" he teases.

"Very funny, smartass," I reply, narrowing my eyes.

"I thought so," he counters.

I shake my head and stare out the window as we turn onto the long street leading to the estate. "What's his mood like today?" I ask because I'm honestly curious.

"Shockingly good," he replies.

"Good like a normal person, or good like Adam?"

Bastian laughs as he turns onto the estate's drive. "He's a good guy," he says, his French accent slipping through.

"How *exactly* did you two meet? You've never totally explained that before?" I inquire because neither of them has told me the whole story.

"In Paris," Bastian responds as we drive through the tunnel of trees.

"I know that but like how? All I know is you two were upset over breakups and he used to hang out at a bar where you worked, but there has to be more to that story."

"I'll let Adam tell you. It's a long story and we've arrived. Let's just say, Adam and I are two scorned lovers whose paths crossed most unusually," he says.

"You're seriously leaving me hanging with that cliffhanger?" I ask.

"Oui," he replies as he parks and gets out to open my door.

I take his offered hand and he helps me out of the car and up the stairs to the enormous front doors. I hesitate when he opens them and motions for me to enter. Call it déjà vu or PTSD, but memories of less than a week ago flood my mind. It's barely been a couple of days since the snowstorm...since I spent three whole days alone with Adam.

I swallow and make the final step into the house. I shiver as Bastian closes the door.

"He's waiting in the ballroom," Bastian says, and I frown.

"There's a ballroom?"

Bastian laughs. "This way."

"Is that Isa?" Mrs. Potter says as she throws open a door to what looks like a small office.

"Hi," I squeak as she pulls me into a hug and then steps back. "Thomas, come look. Doesn't she just look beautiful?"

An older man with a beard like Santa Claus gets up from a desk and walks over to us. "This is my husband, Thomas. Thomas, this is Isa Garren."

"It's a pleasure to meet you, Ms. Garren," Thomas says.

"Likewise, and please call me Isa."

"You're going to have such a great time," Mrs. Potter exclaims.

"I...hope so," I respond because I don't know what else to say, hell, I don't even know what we're doing tonight.

"Come on, Adam hates to wait," Bastian says.

"Adam can wait for a second so I can see this gorgeous dress he picked out," Mrs. Potter scolds as she looks at my dress. "It really is perfect for you. OK, off you go. You have fun now."

"I will. Nice meeting you again, Thomas," I say.

The old man tips his head a little, and before I can say anything else, Bastian grabs my hand to pull me along.

I follow him toward the library. He opens a set of doors before we reach the library and I pause as I take in the enormous room. It's completely void of furniture. There are several paintings on the walls, but it's the ceiling that draws my attention. It's rounded and it's dark blue with little lights dotting it, little stars. Clouds dot the skyscape, and the stars are aligned into the constellations of the summer sky.

"It's breathtaking," I whisper, but my voice echoes around the empty space.

"I couldn't agree more," Adam's voice responds, and I jump a little.

He's standing in the corner nearest me and Bastian. Bastian squeezes my shoulder. "Have a good night, Ms. Garren," he says with a wink before shutting the door, leaving me alone with Bastian.

Adam holds out his hand to me and I slowly take it. "Care to dance?" he asks. I look around in confusion.

"I thought...aren't we going..." I trail off.

He smiles down at me as he pulls me into his arms. "We are. I just thought it'd be nice to have a quiet moment first."

He spins us toward a wall and puts his hand on the wall and a panel opens. He presses some buttons. Suddenly a waltz blares on speakers hidden somewhere in the room. He spins me toward the center, and we dance. I let him lead because I have no idea how to waltz.

"Where are we going tonight?" I ask.

"To the city," he replies.

I furrow my brows as more confusion sets in. "The city... but that's so far away."

"Have you ever ridden in a helicopter?" he asks.

"We're taking a helicopter?"

He nods. "Yes. The helipad just got cleared. It's the only way I travel," he explains.

"The *only* way?" I inquire, hoping he'll elaborate since I'm guessing this stems from the accident that killed his parents.

He grins. "Aside from my horse."

I giggle. "No cars, then?"

He shakes his head slightly. "No cars."

He doesn't elaborate and I decide to not press him on it.

The song finishes and he pulls back but doesn't release my hand. "I want to show you something before we leave."

"OK," I say with a look of skepticism.

He leads me to his room. He points to the staircase. I slowly walk up the stairs and into a room. It's dark and I can't tell what it is.

"What is this?" I ask as I step inside.

I feel the heat of his body behind mine. He flicks on the lights, and I gasp at the mural surrounding us. The room is painted like a forest with dozens of cardinals. It literally looks like a panorama, three hundred and sixty degrees of nature surrounds me. It's gorgeous.

"It's beautiful," I say softly as I step forward to look at the artwork.

"My father had this level of the tower finished for me. I asked my mother to paint something here." He pauses and steps forward to stand next to me where I'm examining a part of the mural that features a nest. "And so, she painted me this."

My jaw drops open. "Your mother painted all of this?" I ask, my voice rising with surprise.

"Yes. She didn't advertise it, but she was a very accomplished painter. All the paintings out in the library are hers," he states as he leans forward to look at one of the birds.

I study his profile in the soft lighting of the room. He's... handsome, very handsome. I'm not sure why I hadn't considered that before. It's not just his piercing blue eyes or well-sculpted body, it's all of him. I turn to look back at the wall, my eyes following a path painted in the mural. I spin wanting to see where it leads. It grows narrower, leading away from the place we stand. In the woods behind the trees, there's a castle and it looks so familiar.

I step toward it and hold out a finger tracing it while not

touching it. "Is this..." I trail off as I study it closer, leaning in until my nose is mere millimeters away.

"It's our home," he says from behind me.

I turn around to face him. He's watching me or is he seeing me? The way he looks at me is like he's staring into my soul. It's unnerving.

"Thank you for sharing this with me," I whisper and then clear my throat, realizing I don't need to lower my voice.

He smiles. "I've never shared it with anyone before."

I feel my heart start to pound in my chest.

"Why me?" I ask, my curiosity getting the best of me.

He reaches out and brushes a stray hair off my face, tucking it behind my ear. I don't step away. I don't want to admit that I like this touch, but I do.

"Because you're real. And I know you'd appreciate it, truly appreciate it."

"Who else knows it's here?" I ask.

"The Potters...and Bastian."

Now my curiosity goes into overdrive. I bite my lower lip to keep myself from asking, but in the end, my need to know prevails. "How exactly did you meet Bastian?"

Adam's eyes dance with both sadness and happiness all at once in a way I didn't think was possible. "I fell in love," he starts.

My eyes widen.

He chuckles. "Not with Bastian."

"Oh," I mutter, feeling my cheeks heat with embarrassment.

"I was in love with a woman. Stephanie. And I followed her to Paris. It was shortly after my parents were killed. Looking back...I don't even know if it really was love, but sure as fuck felt like it at the time. One night, I was working late, and I came home to find her in bed with another man. She swore it was nothing and begged me to forgive her. I did, but I began to have the man followed. Turns out, he was dating someone else too...a man."

Adam pauses and gives me a knowing look and I can feel my mouth drop open.

"No fucking way?" I say.

"Fucking way," Adam replies. "The man was with Bastian. I learned Bastian was a cook and bartender. I visited the restaurant where he worked and struck up a conversation with him. I didn't plan on becoming friends with him, but there was just something about the man. Like...he was meant to be my friend...my brother." Adam pauses as if remembering something and then continues. "Anyhow, let's just say the next time our significant others met up, Bastian found them. He came in the next day to work, told me about it when he saw me, and I fessed up. He was angry at first. I went home and ended my relationship, and so did he. I ended up at the bar drunk the next night and he offered me a couch at his place which was just down the street. We lay on the floor of his living room sharing a very expensive bottle of wine and lamenting about our failed relationships. And when the sun rose that next morning, I asked him to join my staff and move back here with me. I'm not sure why he agreed to such a leap of faith, it was the craziest thing I'd ever done, but here we are, nearly seven years later, and I've never regretted that decision."

I grin at the end of his story. "I'm glad he came here. Bastian is a good man." Adam nods.

"You said you...hate women...is that why?" I ask, feeling brave.

Adam looks away for a long moment and then back at me. "Yes. I promised myself I'd never be vulnerable again. I'd given her everything. I needed her. After my parents died, she was all I had. And then I had nothing. I won't ever put myself in that position again," he explains.

"Ever? But what about Bastian? You trust him," I ask.

"That's different," Adam states. "He's seen me at my worst and was still my friend."

"That's sad," I say as I spin away from Adam.

"Is it?"

"Yes. I know being vulnerable to others is scary, but why live if we can't share our life with the people we grow to love?" I state.

He doesn't reply right away. "Maybe it's better that people don't grow to love me," he answers. But before I can respond, he says, "Come on, the helicopter is waiting. I don't want us to be late."

"Late for what exactly?" I ask as I follow him toward the back of the house.

"The Wellington Family Foundation's annual gala," he says.

My eyes widen. "As in, your family's charity?" I ask as he removes his tuxedo jacket and puts it over my shoulders.

"Yes. Come on, let's be quick. It's cold out," he states as he ushers me toward the helicopter behind the kitchen. Mrs. Potter waves at us from a side door. I wave back as a pilot shuts our door.

I glance over at Adam as he hands me a headset to put on. "I'm your date to *your* gala?" I ask loudly as the helicopter's blades begin to spin.

"You are." He turns toward the pilot who gives us a quick safety rundown before we rise into the night sky, heading toward the city. I watch the lights of our small town grow fainter. I turn to Adam.

"Are you sure this is a good idea?" I ask.

He laughs. "It's the best idea I've had in a long time."

"I'm not so sure about that," I mutter as I see the lights of the city begin to emerge from the darkness in the distance.

CHAPTER FIFTEEN

Adam

Part of me wishes I could have kept her at Wellington Estate, where we could be alone. I like having her all to myself. But I need to appear settled, strong, and stable in front of my board of directors tonight. I don't want anyone to sense even an ounce of weakness in me. I'm already viewed as a loose cannon, a damaged heir to the throne of Wellington Corporation. And they aren't wrong. I am damaged, but I'll be damned if Titan thinks for one moment that he has a chance at dissolving what five generations of Wellingtons have worked toward.

Chaz makes his way through the crowd.

"Bolinger wants to speak with you," he says under his breath as he approaches us.

"Isa Garren, Chaz Yarnell," I introduce my assistant to my date. Chaz's eyes flick over to Isa and back to me and then back to Isa. I watch him assess her. He notices. She's not like the other women that I typically bring to such events. He looks back at me, eyeing me suspiciously.

"Pleasure to meet you. I have to steal your date for a moment," he says.

"I'll come find you in a few minutes. The bar is open. Why don't you go get yourself a drink?" I suggest as I motion to the bar in the corner of the room.

"Oh, of course, do what you need to," she insists, giving me a small smile. I can tell she's a little nervous. This isn't her normal crowd. I can't blame her. She should be nervous. I've brought a lamb to slaughter. Most of these people would chew her up and spit her out. I watch her walk across the room and only drag my gaze away when Chaz clears his throat.

"*She's* new," he states with a raised eyebrow.

I glare at him. "Where's Bolinger?" I inquire.

"This way," Chaz says as he leads me to a table in the corner of the room.

Karl Bolinger starts yammering on about something irrelevant the second he sees me. He's nearly ninety years old and I question whether he should even be on the board any longer. But he was close to my parents and his loyalty to them is something I continually remind myself of during these types of conversations.

I keep darting my gaze behind him to where I can see Isa standing at the bar. She's now talking to someone, and when they turn toward me, I feel the anger bubbling inside of me like lava in a volcano that's ready to explode.

Jace Baskins is talking to Isa and she's motherfucking laughing. I don't like anything about this. I don't like that she's talking to one of Titan's executives. I don't like that she's talking to a man that nearly ruined my life. And I really don't like that she's talking to another man, period.

"Karl, I need to check on my date. Let's find time next

week to talk more about this," I say, cutting off the older gentleman as I stand and begin walking toward Isa.

I can hear the woman I've tasked with running the charity auction this evening asking Cruz a question. I keep on walking, ignoring what I normally would be listening to. I'm across the room in a matter of seconds.

"Adam, how are you?" Jace asks as I approach him.

"I'm fine. Just here to escort my date to our table," I growl as I place a hand on Isa's lower back. Isa's proximity is the only thing keeping me from pummeling Jace.

She looks up at me with confusion. "It was nice to see you, Jace."

"Great seeing you as well, Isa. I'll stop by the library next week to check out that new book," he says. I watch his eyes flick down to her breasts.

"This way, Isa," I state from behind clenched teeth.

Thankfully, Isa starts moving before I decide to deck Jace for eyeing my date.

"A friend of yours?" Isa quips as we walk.

"Not exactly," I mutter as I press my hand flatly on the skin revealed on her back.

"You don't say," she responds.

I don't have to look down to know she's rolling her eyes. I would explain it now, but I don't want to cause a scene and I also don't want to explain how I know Jace. Or how Jace followed us to the States after he dumped Stephanie. He tried to win Bastian back, but Bastian had already met Max, thankfully. Yeah, Jace is the man who nearly ruined me by sleeping with my ex.

"Why are you this way?" I ask as I wave at a couple I know and give them my best fake smile.

"Why are *you* this way?" she retorts.

I stop walking and look down at her. "I have my reasons," I state.

She bites her red-stained lip. "I know you do," she says, surprising me. Does she know? I highly doubt that.

"This is our table," I state as I motion to the seats in front of us at the main table.

I pull out a seat for Isa and she sits. I assist her in scooting in her chair and my hand touches her shoulder. I see goose bumps form on her arm.

"Are you cold?" I ask as I lean down, my lips near her ear.

"No...I'm fine," she manages and then quickly grabs a flute of champagne in front of her and takes a sip. I smirk. She *is* still affected by me.

I'm about to comment when Cruz comes over to usher me on stage. "I have to go and give a speech. Will you be alright here for a few minutes?" I ask her.

She nods and tips her champagne glass at me. "I'll be fine," she assures me.

I follow Cruz to the stage. The room goes quiet.

"Thank you all for being here this evening," I begin as I look around the room, my eyes finally landing on Isa. "My parents were lovers of many things, but one thing they both enjoyed was reading. Both my parents instilled a love of books in me from an early age." The crowd is filled with murmurs. I typically don't share such personal details, but with Isa here tonight, I feel compelled to stray from my planned speech. I can see Cruz's eyes widen as I continue, "This year's donations from our gala will go toward several grants to increase access to books for children at schools and in libraries around the country, along with programs aimed to help students who struggle with reading due to learning disabilities. I hope you will all open your pocketbooks and share your success with those who are less fortunate. Enjoy the evening, and thank you for your generosity. The Wellington Foundation thanks you as well as we continue our mission to provide our community and beyond with important resources and opportunities."

I pause and there's a round of applause. With a nod of my head, I introduce one of my executives who will be running the charity auction. I head off stage and back to Isa after stopping at a few tables to shake hands.

I can feel Isa watching me, and when I sit down, she places her hand on my arm. I turn to face her and see unshed tears in her eyes.

"Are you alright?" I ask, concern taking hold of me as I look into her eyes.

She gives a wet laugh. "Yes. I...I didn't realize what the auction funds were going to tonight. Your speech was...I think it's wonderful what your charity does," she says.

I smile down at her and take her hand in mine. "You're the one who does the real work, Isa."

She frowns. "Real work?"

"I read your proposal," I state.

Her eyes widen. "You did?"

Nodding, I'm interrupted as my executive toasts me. I raise my glass and then stand and give a little bow as everyone toasts me. Isa raises her glass to me as well, but I sense her reasons are different than the other people in the room. I had read her grant proposal. Last night, I opened that email she had sent so many weeks ago. The grant is from a charity we funded about five years ago. I haven't told her that. But I was impressed with what she's been able to do with her library on a shoestring budget. She's an important member of the Storyview Falls community and her programs have helped hundreds of children.

I sit back down, and Cruz asks me a question, pulling my attention away from Isa for a moment. When I turn back, she's chatting with the woman sitting next to her, the wife of another one of my executives. I watch her for a long moment.

She seems relaxed and confident as she talks about a book, something that was on a bestseller's list last week.

The auction begins and I watch as Isa claps and laughs along with the other attendees. I catch her gaze a few times and we exchange smiles. I like seeing her happy. I was worried she'd feel out of her element here, but I misjudged her. I was so very wrong, about so many things.

The auction winds down and the band starts to play. I hold out my hand to Isa.

"May I have a dance?" I ask.

"Of course," she replies as she places her hand in mine. I lead her out to the center of the dance floor and spin her around. She giggles as I pull her back into my arms.

"You look beautiful tonight," I whisper against the shell of her ear.

She blushes. "Thank you," she says quietly and then looks down at her gown. "The gown, shoes, hair, makeup, is all...you didn't have to do that."

"I know I didn't have to, but I wanted to. Thank you for agreeing to join me tonight," I state as I move us around the dance floor. She doesn't fight my lead for once and something about that makes me feel as if I've gained a little of her trust. I hope I have.

"This was...not what I expected," she admits.

"Oh? What did you expect?" I ask.

Her cheeks turn a dark shade of pink again. "Uh...not this," she says as she motions around us with her hand.

"A gala?" I ask. But I know the answer. She didn't know it was *my* gala and she certainly didn't realize what this fundraiser was for tonight.

I've kept so much from her. I want to protect her, even if that means protecting her from myself.

Part of me so desperately wants to keep her. I shouldn't make her mine. But maybe...maybe there's a way.

I swallow as she shakes her head at my question. "I didn't know it was *your* gala," she confirms.

I look around us, suddenly wanting her to myself. "Let's head home," I suggest as I lead us off the dance floor and let Cruz know I'm departing. The evening is almost over, and after all, it's my event, I can leave when I want. And right now, I want to leave with Isa.

CHAPTER SIXTEEN

Isa

He takes his jacket off my shoulders as I stand in front of the fireplace in the library. "I apologize for not thinking to order you a shawl," he states, his hands running down my bare arms.

"It's alright. I wasn't that cold," I lie. While the temperature is in the upper forties today, it was cold, but I didn't exactly own a jacket or shawl that would go with this dress. I turn to face him and see the look of concern on his face.

This man confuses the hell out of me. I swore he was embarrassed to have been caught with me after the snowstorm and now I feel like he's treating me as though I'm the most precious thing in the world. It feels like that night we shared in his bedroom. The memory of that night heats my cheeks and I swirl back toward the fire.

His large hands come to rest on my exposed shoulders. I can feel the warmth of his body behind mine, and something about that feels like home. He feels like home. That thought jars me and I feel my body tense. He quickly removes his hands as if his touch has caused me discomfort. I want to scream for him to keep them there, that I like the way his skin feels against mine, but I chicken out and stay silent.

"Would you like some scotch?" he asks.

I nod. "Yes, that would be nice. Thank you," I say as I watch the mesmerizing flames lick at the stone tiles on the inside of the fireplace.

I hear him clinking glasses and I know he's at the small hidden bar near the sitting area. I turn toward him as he walks over with two glasses in his hand. I accept one of the fine crystal tumblers.

"To a wonderful evening," he says as he taps his glass against mine.

I raise mine and we both take a long sip of the scotch. His eyes don't leave mine, and damn, I feel the intensity of his gaze.

"Did you enjoy yourself?" he asks as he takes a seat and leans back in the chair, placing his ankle on his opposite knee. He's undone his bowtie and his top two buttons are undone. And he's back to looking like a cover model on a billionaire romance.

I sit on the edge of the seat opposite him, holding my glass in my lap. "I did. It was nice. I didn't expect to know anyone."

If looks could kill, I'd be very afraid of dying right now.

"How do you know Jace?" he asks.

I swallow because I'm feeling like I way underestimated how much Adam loathes Jace.

"H-he is just a patron of the library," I stammer before taking a gulp of scotch and feeling it burn as it slides down my throat.

"Is he a regular *patron* of your library?" Adam asks. His jaw is so clenched, I'm surprised he can speak.

"He doesn't come by any more often than my other patrons," I assure him.

His jaw unclenches slightly. "I see."

"I feel like there's a story there," I state.

His jaw re-clenches and I let out a long breath. This man's anger is like a furnace that's overheated and ready to blow.

He cracks his neck. "Remember I told you how I met Bastian?"

"Yes...your girlfriend..." I trail off as his knowing eyes wait for me to put two and two together.

"No," I whisper.

"Yes," he affirms. "Jace Baskins stole my girlfriend and broke Bastian's heart in the process."

"Fuck," I mutter under my breath.

"Yeah," he agrees.

"I...I swear I didn't know that," I say as I look into his eyes. I'm not sure why I want him to know that, but I do. I want this man to trust me. The more little pieces he's revealed to me, the more I feel like he's a wounded animal and not a pompous rich asshole. His parents, his girlfriend, and his whole life have been about loss for the past fifteen years. I can't begin to imagine how he must feel.

His features soften. "I know. How could you have possibly known that? Jace doesn't exactly come to our little town often. When he has business, he comes and then he immediately goes..." Adam trails off and I feel like there's more he's not saying.

"'Cause you told him to?" I guess with a raised eyebrow.

"In not so many words. Yes," he confirms.

"I see. That explains why I don't see him that often," I muse as I consider his periodic visits to the library. It's typically to use a private conference room and I always wondered why someone so well-dressed didn't keep an office in town, but now it makes much more sense.

I finish my drink and stand. "I should...get home. I need to let Felipe out," I announce because if I don't get out of here soon, I'm afraid I'll give in to my desire to kiss him, and if I kiss him, I'll remember how it felt to have him worshipping my body, and if I remember that...well, I'll just wind up alone and hurt when this is all over.

"Oh, uh, alright, then. I'll call Bastian to take you home," he says.

"I can just call a car," I say with a little laugh.

Adam stands and steps toward me, his huge frame towering over mine. "Bastian will take you."

"No need. I can take care of myself," I huff as I try to step around him.

His hand comes out and lands on my shoulder and I look up at him once more. He doesn't look angry, he looks...worried?

"Please, Isa. Let me have Bastian take you home. I'll feel better knowing he drove you rather than some random stranger," he insists.

I turn back to him. His thumb caresses my arm before he drops his hand to his side. "Why don't you take me?" I ask because I want him to tell me. I want him to explain it. I want to hear it from him.

"Come back tomorrow and...I'll explain then," he says as he pulls out his phone and sends a text. "Bastian's pulling the car around now."

I look up at him with curiosity. I want to ask if this is date number two. Didn't he say over four weeks? But I decide not to press him, at least not right now. "What time tomorrow?"

"Are you working?" he asks.

I shrug. "I could work every day. Right now, I have two part-time staff and two volunteers, but I prefer to be there as much as I can. If I can get the furnace fixed, we'll be open," I explain.

"Do you need me to call someone to fix it?" he asks.

"Nope. Already on top of that," I say, trying not to let my pride get the better of me. After all, he's trying to be nice.

"Then text me when you finish with your work," he says.

"OK," I reply as I turn and head toward the front hall.

I find Bastian waiting for me.

"Your chariot awaits," he says with a swoop of his hand and a slight bow.

I roll my eyes. "You are seriously deranged," I mutter as he opens the door and then pulls out something from a hidden closet.

"Adam insisted I give this to you," he says with a roll of his eyes as he hands me an antique fur shawl.

I giggle. "Uh, thanks?" I say as I take it and put it over my shoulders. It's late and I'm tired. But mostly I'm confused. I went into this evening with an "all business" attitude and now...I don't know what I feel. Fine, I know what I feel, but I don't want to feel it. I'm afraid of these feelings, afraid they won't be reciprocated.

Bastian rattles on about how we already made the entertainment news and even tosses me his cell phone so I can see the photos from the gala that are in an article about Adam Wellington's surprise date, who is she and are they together?

"Great, just what I need, unwanted publicity," I groan.

"Hey, all publicity is good publicity," Adam says.

"You're kidding, right?"

"No, maybe you can milk some of those rich people for money. You told Elisha you wanted to buy the old Bradley property on Crestwood Drive," he says.

"I guess. But right now, I just want to go home, put on pajamas and go to sleep," I say with a yawn as Bastian pulls up to my apartment. I laugh when I see Felipe in the window.

"Why do you own a horse? He's totally impractical," Bastian scoffs as he parks the car.

"So are those leather shoes that you're wearing, yet you

have them on anyhow," I tease as I open the door. "Thanks for the ride," I add with a wave as I head up to my apartment.

I open my door and am greeted by total destruction.

"Felipe!" I screech. Then I look around and let out a groan. He's completely trashed my apartment. Pieces of fluff from my pillows lie on the sofa. He's managed to knock over a small bookshelf and books are strewn everywhere. He's chewed up a wooden spoon and the plastic handle of a saucepan.

He stops chewing on the pillow he has between his paws and tilts his head as if surprised to see me.

"Buddy! What the hell?" I say as I start picking things up.

My phone rings and I pull it out of my pocket. "You got home alright?" Adam asks before I can speak.

"Uh, yeah, why?" I ask with a frown.

"Just making sure. Bastian said he waited till you were inside, but I know you have to go up the stairs and I just wanted to make sure..." He trails off.

I huff as I pull out a garbage bag and start throwing things away, things I can't afford to replace. I groan when I hear a vibration.

I turn my head and drop the phone, running to grab my vibrator out of Felipe's mouth.

"Drop it!" I yell.

Felipe thinks it's a game and goes running through the apartment with my pink rabbit vibrator in his mouth. "Felipe! So help me! Drop the vibrator or I will turn you into a rug!"

I look around and see his favorite chew toy and pick it up. Felipe immediately drops the vibrator and runs to me, grabbing the red toy and settling at my feet.

I race back to my phone and pick it up. "Sorry about that," I say as I catch my breath.

"Is everything alright over there?" Adam says in an amused voice.

"It's...sort of. Felipe got bored and destroyed my apart-ment," I state as I go to grab my vibrator which now has teeth marks all over it.

"Ew," I mutter, turning it off and dropping it in my drawer. I'll deal with that later. I don't have money to replace it. Elisha bought it as a birthday gift and I looked it up, that thing is like one hundred dollars. It *was* my favorite one. Anyhow, it's amazing and I'm so worked up, I could really use it right now.

"Stupid dog," I huff.

"That does not sound OK," Adam says.

"I'm sorry. I'm just going to get cleaned up and go to bed. This was not how I wanted my evening to end," I explain.

"I'll see you tomorrow evening, Isa. Sweet dreams," Adam says.

"Goodnight," I reply as I disconnect. I toss the garbage bag down. And take off my dress, hanging it carefully in the closet and making sure the door is closed so Felipe can't destroy it. Then I shower and head to bed. Maybe a good night of sleep will fix all my problems.

CHAPTER SEVENTEEN

Adam

I've been pacing in my office for three hours. I decided to pick Isa up myself today.

"Hey, how was the gala?" Bastian asks as he knocks at the same time, he pokes his head inside my office.

I glare at him, and he gives me his innocent smile. "Have I told you lately that you are annoying as fuck?"

"Twice this morning. Clearly, that wasn't enough," he says with a grin. "So? How was it?"

"It was good. We raised five million dollars between the auction and the matches."

"Wow! That's great, but we both know I was referring to Isa," Bastian says, giving me a pointed look.

I sit down and Bastian sits on the arm of one of my wing-backed chairs, which he knows annoys the fuck out of me.

"It went well. I'm picking her up this evening for another date," I explain.

"What exactly is the end goal of these *dates*?" he asks.

"I...well, I did have a dinner with some clients tonight, but it got canceled, so I thought we could go horseback riding," I explain, trying to dodge his actual question.

"So...do you like her?" Bastian asks.

"Yes. Of course, I like her."

"But do you, *like* like her," he prods.

"Oh, leave Mr. Wellington alone, you nosy man," Mrs. Potter says from the door as she knocks and brings a tray in with some tea and cookies. It's a habit she's long had since I was a boy. I haven't been able to stop her from doing it.

"Oh come on, Petunia, you know you are dying to know too!" Bastian exclaims as he walks over and grabs a cookie from the tray. Mrs. Potter slaps his hand but he manages to take one.

"It's none of my business what Mr. Wellington does with his personal life." She looks at me with a warm smile and pats my arm. "I just like seeing you happy, my dear."

"Thank you," I say to her, returning her smile. She's the closest thing I have left to a mother, and I adore her.

"You said your dinner meeting in the city got canceled. Will you be eating here this evening?" she asks.

"I think we might," I say as I look at Bastian. He smirks.

"What shall I make you lovebirds?" he asks.

"What? You actually are going to ask me?" I question.

He shrugs.

"I will text you a menu with something I have in mind and I also have another errand for you to run," I add with a smirk.

He raises an eyebrow. I had heard Isa yelling at Felipe last night. It sounds like the dog ate her vibrator, so I think Bastian will need to run out and buy a new one. Then I consider it. Fuck, he'll probably enjoy it, knowing him.

"Mrs. Potter, can you get Mr. Potter to get Apollo and Cleo saddled up for me? I'm going to pick up Isa," I say.

She nods and leaves. Bastian looks at me. "I could drive you?" he suggests, his demeanor becoming serious for a moment.

"It's alright. I'd rather ride," I state.

"It's not far," Bastian urges. I know he wants me to get back in a car, but I just can't do it. I've taken my helicopter and then the subway for years now or I've ridden my horse into town on the very rare occasions I've had to go there. It's limited my ability to travel and do the things I used to love doing, but every time I get in a car, I feel the panic set in. My therapist says it's PTSD and that eventually I may be able to overcome it. But I'm not so sure about that.

I send Bastian directions a minute after he leaves my office. And ten seconds later, he's back inside.

"You want me to get what?" he says loudly.

"Steaks, fondant potatoes, asparagus with a hollandaise sauce," I state as I try to keep myself from smirking.

"And?" Bastian prods.

"Oh, and some baked brie with your cranberry jam for dessert, maybe a nice port to go with that," I state.

"You're an asshole. You know that?" Bastian says. "You know that's not what I was talking about. Why are you sending me on *your* sex errands."

"It's not a sex errand," I state matter-a-factly.

"D'accord," he says with a sigh.

"Her dog chewed up hers. I wanted to surprise her with a new one," I explain.

"So, you don't plan on using this as part of your *date* tonight?" he asks, making air quotes when he says "date."

"No, that's not my *plan*," I answer.

He mutters in French under his breath and leaves me. I let the smirk I've been holding inside release. I love bothering him. I'd never admit how much his friendship has meant to me and he'd never bring it up, but damn, I love him like the brother I never had.

I scroll through some contracts and some possible real estate investments. If I can just find a few more, I can keep James Titan at bay. My eyes land on a piece of property here in Storyview Falls. I've been eyeing it for a while. It's an old farm that abuts the downtown area. The house itself is massive and old and it's near the road and walkable to Main Street, but there isn't a reason for me to keep it. I've been looking for the perfect property for one of the companies I want to acquire. I envision a sort of walkable campus. I send Cruz my thoughts on this and ask him to look into it.

There's a knock at the door and Bastian is standing there smiling. He walks like he's on a goddamn runway, strutting across the room, and drops a pink bag on my desk.

"Your vibrator, sir," he says with a flourish of his hand.

I give him a pointed look.

"Does sir need anything else?" he asks.

"Fuck off and get to work on dinner. I'd like to eat promptly at eight," I state.

"Very well," he says and struts back out of my office. I run a hand over my face. Glancing at the time, I realize I need to get my riding clothes on. I text Isa.

Me: Wear something warm and comfortable.

Isa: Aye aye, Captain.

Me: Very funny.

Isa: I thought so.

Me: Do you enjoy torturing me?

Isa: (thinking emoji) Yes.

Me: Noted.

Isa: (kissing emoji)

"Well, I do hope there's a message with good news. And from the look on your face, I'd say there most definitely is," Mrs. Potter's voice rings out from my doorway.

"I...uh...just a real estate prospect," I stammer as I put my phone down.

"Oh?" she asks, her eyes knowing. I can't hide shit from that woman.

"I'm going to go get Isa," I say as I stand and walk toward her.

When I reach the door, Mrs. Potter grabs my arm and I stop.

"I know...the last decade has been...hard for you. But since Isa's been in your life, I see that spark in your eye again. Things *can* be different, Adam. Your parents would want you to be happy. They'd want you to live again. There are *good* women out there and Isa is one of them. Remember that," she says, patting my arm as she pulls her hand away.

"I should get back to the kitchen to help Bastian. Thomas has the horses ready when you are," she says.

Nodding, I walk to the main staircase and up to my room. My mind is on Isa the entire time. Is Mrs. Potter right? Can I be happy again? I haven't been truly happy in so long, I don't even know if that's possible.

I get changed and go out to the stables. The snow has begun melting, which means I can use the trail to get into town. I pat Apollo's neck and he noses my pocket. I pull out a carrot that I grabbed on my way out.

"You spoil him," Thomas grunts. I grin. As sweet as Petunia is, Thomas is equally curmudgeonly. But I also know he's all bark and no bite. He's a softie on the inside.

"'Cause he's a good boy, aren't you, Apollo?" I run my hand down his soft nose, and he grunts his response.

"See, even Apollo knows he's a good boy."

"Do you want Cleo tied to Apollo or do you want to hold her reins?" he asks.

"I'll hold them," I say as I get up on Apollo. He hands me her reins and steps back.

"You've been going to town quite a bit lately," he says.

Shrugging, I nudge Apollo to start walking. "Just have some business to attend to," I say vaguely.

"Is that what the kids call it nowadays?" Thomas mutters.

I chuckle and get the horses moving in a canter toward the trail. A few miles later, I move us through a bit of uncleared snow at the small park behind Flagstaff Road and then I turn onto Main Street. It's a slow evening. Only a few cars dot the thoroughfare. I stop in front of Elisha's bakery. Before I even have the horses tied up, Elisha is standing on the sidewalk.

"Do not fuck around with Isa," she says. Her eyes might as well be shooting flames at me.

I hold up my hands. "I thought I made it clear. I would never hurt Isa."

"I don't like this whole *arrangement* you have going," she says, eyeing me suspiciously.

"Understood," I say as I step around her to ring the bell for Isa's apartment.

"Just remember, I have a shovel," she says as the door buzzer sounds and I open it.

"Yeah, I haven't forgotten," I tell her. I hurry up the stairs and the door flies open. I find Isa in a pair of jeans, a cream sweater, a scarf, and a hat.

Felipe sees me and bounds over, nearly knocking me down. "Hey, Felipe," I say as I scratch his head as he leans all one hundred and fifty pounds of his weight against me.

"You ready?" I ask.

"Sure," she says as she eyes me with curiosity. "Do I need to bring anything else?"

"Does Felipe like nature walks? He can tag along if you like. Is he OK to be off leash?" I ask, realizing I don't want her using Felipe as an excuse to leave me early.

"Oh. Uh, sure. Let me just get his lead in case I need it."

She grabs a lead and puts some sort of ridiculous dog coat on Felipe who stares at me pathetically. I give him a look that says, "Sorry, buddy. I can't help you with this one."

"All set," she says as she slides her phone into her pocket.

They follow me outside and she looks at Apollo and Cleo. "Uh, how am I supposed to get up there?" she asks, looking around as if I may have brought steps.

I grin. "Come here," I command. I place my hands on her waist and place her up on top of Cleo, who for the record is not that large of a horse. Although with Isa sitting up on top of her, she does seem bigger than she is.

"Do you know how to ride?" I ask, frowning as I hadn't thought about that before this very moment.

"Oh, sort of," Isa says. I give her a quick tutorial and then we head down to the end of the block and start on the trail. Felipe happily walks beside us.

"I never come back here," Isa says as we meander the path.

"I hadn't been back here in ages...before the other day," I state.

"It's pretty," she adds as she looks around us at the barren trees, stone outcroppings, and frozen waterfalls of the stream that runs alongside us.

"I suppose it is," I agree.

"You suppose?" she laughs.

"Fine. It's pretty," I agree.

She rolls her eyes and shakes her head. "You, Adam Wellington, need to enjoy life more often."

"Is that so?"

She nods. "Let's race back to your house!" she says and then frowns as if trying to remember something. "How do I? What's her name again?" She pats Cleo.

"That's Cleo," I say. "She's older and sweeter than Apollo.

You could probably get her to canter but I'm not sure she'll gallop."

Isa grins devilishly and I realize a second too late that she's going to try. She nudges Cleo and then again and the two of them go sprinting ahead. Felipe barks and chases after them.

"Wait up! There's a downed...tree." I say the last word two seconds too late because Cleo leaps over the tree and Isa goes sailing. Fuck.

I bring Apollo to a screeching halt and jump off, running toward Isa, who's planted face-first into the snow.

"Isa!" I yell as I reach her and roll her over, only to find she's laughing.

"Isa?" I ask, my hands roaming over my body, looking for injury.

"I'm...fine," she manages as she laughs.

"Here, let me help you up," I say as I reach for her elbow to help her stand.

"Ouch," she mutters once she gets on two feet.

"What? Where are you hurt?" I ask, my brows furrowing as I look over her body again for injuries.

"I think I twisted my ankle. I'll survive," she says. But before she even finishes the sentence, I swoop her into my arms and carry her over to Apollo. I help her to sit on his saddle and then I climb on behind her. I pull her back against me. It's not ideal but it'll do.

"Hold on," I say as I wrap an arm around her waist, keeping her flush against me. Felipe nudges our feet with his nose and whines.

"I'm fine, buddy," she assures him.

"We'll take it slow from here," I say into her ear.

She shivers against me.

"We're almost back and we'll get you all warmed up," I say as Apollo trots toward the house.

"I'm fine, Adam. Really, it's just a little ankle twist and my pride...mostly my pride," she says, but I want to examine her ankle myself.

We make it back in a few minutes and Thomas greets us at the front door, holding Cleo's lead.

"You kids alright?" he asks, frowning.

"Yes, we're fine. Cleo just got overzealous and jumped a downed tree," I explain as I stop Apollo and help Isa down.

"Cleo must have wanted to impress you. She normally doesn't jump things anymore. She's an old lady," he says with a laugh as he pats Cleo's side. Isa hobbles over to Cleo and Cleo pulls back a little.

"I'm alright, Cleo. It's OK," she says softly as she holds out a hand. I reach into my pocket and hand her two sugar cubes and she feeds them to Cleo who greedily eats them. I turn and give Apollo a few as well.

When I look back, Isa is stroking Cleo's neck.

"You don't have to impress me, Cleo. Us ladies have to stick together now, don't we?" she says softly. Cleo lets out a little whinny. Thomas laughs.

"I think Miss Cleo here likes you quite a bit. Maybe don't try taking her over any walls or trees, but I think she'd like to go out riding again sometime," Thomas says to Isa.

"I'd like that," Isa replies with a smile.

"Come on, let's go look at your ankle. Can you take these two knuckleheads back to the stables for me?" I ask Thomas. He nods.

"Nice seeing you, Isa," Thomas adds as I open the door and help Isa inside.

"Let's get your ankle soaking in some Epsom salts," I say as I pick Isa up in my arms and carry her up to my room.

"It's really not necessary," Isa protests, but then she wraps her arms tightly around my neck. I like this, Isa in my arms.

I reluctantly set her on the end of my tub, and I see her

blush as she looks at it. The memories of what we did in here are thick in the air as I fill the tub with water and salts. I help Isa remove her boots. Her ankle doesn't look too bad, which is a good sign.

She rolls up her jeans and lets me set her foot in the tub.

I open a cabinet and find some painkillers and hand her one with a cup of water.

"Thank you," she murmurs as she sets the glass down.

"You're welcome," I say, frowning as I realize just how hurt she could have been.

"Sit down. I'm fine, you can relax now," Isa encourages as she pats the side of the tub next to her. I sit down and look into her eyes. Eyes I've become intimately familiar with lately. I brush some hair away from her face.

"Are you cold?" I ask.

She shakes her head. "No, I'm good."

"I have Bastian making us some steaks and potatoes and brie," I say.

"Sounds good. I thought we had dinner with someone tonight. Is this our second *date*?" she asks, cocking her head to one side.

"We did. But the meeting got canceled, so I thought maybe we could just hang out anyhow, since I suppose this is the second date," I say.

"Oh...you didn't want to use your second date for a meeting or gala or something?" she asks. I want to scream, "No, I just want to spend time with you," but I decide to play it cool.

"I thought we could talk more about the library and your grant," I lie.

"Oh, uh, sure," she says.

"Adam?" she asks.

"Yes."

"I... never mind," she says, looking away.

I take her chin in my hand and turn her face back toward me. "What?" I ask, our lips only inches apart.

"I..." she starts again but the intercom buzzes.

"Mr. Wellington, dinner will be served in fifteen minutes in the dining hall," Bastian says. Fucking Bastian and his horrible timing.

CHAPTER EIGHTEEN

Isa

I clear my throat and look back at my ankle. "I feel much better," I say as I start to stand. Adam grabs a towel and helps me dry off my foot before slowly rolling my sock back up my foot and sliding my boot back on it.

He takes my hand and leads me to the dining hall. This time, we're sitting side by side. Well, that's different. There's a gift bag sitting by what I assume is my place at the table.

"What's this?" I ask.

He grins. "A small gift for you."

I open it and pull out...a vibrator? Damn, a really, really nice one.

"Uh...thanks?" I squeak as I quickly place it back in the bag.

"It sounded like Felipe might have eaten one of yours," he says with a wink.

I blush. "Yeah, that *may* have happened."

"We can try that one out later," he adds as he leans in and

kisses the space just below my earlobe. Christ! This man is dangerous. Suddenly, I don't want dinner, I want him.

"Filet mignon, blanched asparagus in a hollandaise sauce, and fondant potatoes. And for dessert, I've brought out the baked brie and homemade baguette as requested," Bastian says as he comes in with plates in his hand. I look over to see Adam glaring at him. Wait, Adam requested this? That's interesting.

"Thanks, Bastian. This looks amazing. And thank Mrs. Potter, I know she was back there helping you," I say.

He smiles. "Will do," he says as Isaac and Ames come running into the room followed by Felipe.

"I swear to God, I fed those beasts," Bastian says with a sigh.

"I know. Thank you, Bastian. You can head home. I'll call if I need you," Adam says. Bastian nods and gives me another wink and I roll my eyes as he takes his exit. He stops at the door and turns back to us.

"Enjoy that gift, Isa. Let's just say, Adam sent me on an errand to get it. It is the top of the line and has more settings than the International Space Station," he adds with a laugh as he leaves.

My face turns red as I turn to Adam. He just shrugs.

The dogs sit down next to Adam and wag their tails. Even Felipe does it which makes me laugh.

"I take it your dogs enjoy steak?" I ask.

"Clearly they have good taste," he replies, turning toward me as he takes a bite. I watch the fork slide between his lips. Why is that so erotic? Why am I getting overheated by Adam eating? What the hell is wrong with me? This is still just a business transaction, right? Adam doesn't want to be with someone like me. He made that perfectly clear before.

I turn back to my food and cut my steak. When I taste it, I can't help moaning. It's the best steak I've ever had. I chew with my eyes closed, savoring it. When I open them, I find Adam watching my mouth.

I blush. "That steak is amazing. I can't believe Max hasn't stolen Bastian away to work at his restaurant."

"He tried once," Adam admits.

"And?"

"And he lost," Adam answers.

"He lost? What does that even mean?"

"I challenged him to a game of basketball because he thought I couldn't play, and he lost," Adam says with a shrug.

"You pool sharked him with basketball?" I ask, my voice rising an octave.

"I think you just made pool shark a verb. And yes, I suppose. I let him pick how we'd compete. He just didn't choose wisely."

"Right," I reply with a laugh as I take another bite of steak.

"So, tell me about your library. We've spoken about mine, but not yours," Adam says as he digs into his potatoes.

"Well, I started working there after college. Storyview Falls has had a library of its own since...wait, you should know this," I say as I eye him suspiciously.

"But it's more fun to have you tell me," he says with a smirk.

I roll my eyes. "Fine. Since your great-great-grandfather gifted part of his book collection along with several hundred dollars and space on Main Street in a building he owned. When he died, the building went into a trust held for the library. So, we at least don't have to pay rent. But we do have utilities, electronics, new books, and such. In a small town, it's hard to keep it going. We do an annual fundraiser, but it usually is just enough for us to get by, not for all the things I'd love to do," I explain.

"Such as?" he prods.

"I'd love more community spaces, free classes, reading help for kids, more computers, and activities for the kids on the weekend and during the summer," I say before taking another bite of my dinner.

"And you can't do all that now?"

I shake my head. "Sometimes, I can offer a free class and we did get gifted a computer from..." I trail off as I realize he won't like what I have to say.

"Jace?" he asks.

I blush and nod slowly. "As I said, he's a good patron of the library."

"Hmmm..." Adam says.

"Oh, come on, you can't be threatened by him, he's just... Jace," I say as if he's some little old man who stops to read mysteries on Tuesdays, which we do have.

"What about your parents?" he asks.

I pause. "I love them, they are great people, but I would never ask them for money. It would be...like I failed," I admit.

"Now, that, I can understand."

"I mean, I let them buy raffle prizes at our booth at the annual winter festival, but I don't let on to them about how financially tough it is," I explain.

"But you'll tell me?"

Shrugging, I take the last bite on my plate. I consider his question while I chew. "Well, I already asked you for the books, so you know I need a grant. And..." I want to say that I trust him, but do I?

"And?"

"And...you're a businessman, so you get it," I say, chickening out.

I watch Adam give each dog a small piece of meat before shooing them off to sit by the fireplace.

"You're good with animals," I say.

He pauses and looks at me. "I was an only child. My pets

were like my siblings. We played together. Hell, Apollo and I grew up together."

I grin. "You're a closet softy, aren't you?"

"No," he says sharply, which only makes me giggle.

"That's what a grumpy sunshine character would say," I tease.

"A what?"

"You know, in a romance story where the male character appears grumpy, but he's not really grumpy."

"I don't read romance," he says deadpan.

"That's what people who read romance always say," I quip as I break off a piece of baguette and lather it with brie.

"You're impossible," he grumbles as he grabs a piece of bread for himself.

"Whatever you say, Mr. Grumpy Sunshine," I say with a wink.

Isaac comes over and sits by Adam again.

"Paw," Adam says. Isaac lifts his paw.

"High five," Adam commands. Isaac gives him a high five.

"Low five." Then, "Fist Bump."

"Impressive skills," I say to Isaac.

Adam gives him some bread with brie on it and Isaac wags his little stub of a tail happily.

I lean back in my chair and analyze this enigma of a man next to me. He has wonderful staff who are friendly, funny, and kind. Even his assistant, Cruz, seems cool. He loves his animals. Yet, when it comes to women, he's...afraid of commitment and perhaps afraid to get hurt again? So, does he want to remain a playboy with his sex-toy closet forever?

"Why are you staring at me like that?" he asks.

"Like what?"

"Like you're trying to see if I have any neurons firing in my brain." He gives me a quizzical look.

I purse my lips before answering. "Just trying to figure you out."

"Good luck with that," he mutters.

I take one last sip of my wine. "What shall we do now?" I ask as I look around us.

"Are you kids all done?" Mrs. Potter says from the doorway.

I jump and clutch my chest. "You scared me!" I yelp and then smile at her.

"I'm sorry, my dear. I'm here to clear the table," she says with a warm mischievous smile.

"Or...you're spying on us," Adam calls her bluff.

Her grin widens. "Maybe," she says as she places our plates on a wheeling cart. "Can I get you kids anything else, or shall I exit the room before you use the table for other festivities?" she asks.

"Petunia," Adam grumbles, his cheeks turning a little red.

I laugh. "We're all done, Mrs. Potter. And I am not sure about the table, but who knows, maybe later," I add with a wink.

She pats the wooden tabletop. "Thomas and I have enjoyed many a night on our kitchen table. Never underestimate a good, solid wood table." She pauses and looks at Adam. I've never seen this man get exasperated before, but right now, he looks like he wants to sink into the floor. "Anything else, Mr. Wellington?"

"That'll be all, Mrs. Potter," he says from behind clenched teeth.

She smiles. "Have a nice evening. I'm going to take care of these dishes and head home," she says to us, giving me one more wink on her way out the door.

I lean toward Adam. "Do you think she's been drinking? She's so...sassy tonight," I ask as I look back toward the door to the kitchen.

Adam laughs. "She can be...*sassy* but she's never been quite this *sassy* before."

"Well, good for her and Mr. Potter. Their senior sex life seems epic," I mutter.

Adam looks at me. "And yours isn't?"

I give him a credulous look. "I'm a librarian."

"And?" he prods.

"I live above a bakery café with a giant dog," I add.

"So?"

"So, men aren't exactly swooping in to date me. And I'm definitely not going on an app to swipe right."

"What about Jace?" he asks.

I look at the table. "Do you think Jace would do it on a table with me?" I ask.

I'm about to tell him Jace isn't really my type, but he swoops me up and deposits me on top of the table right in front of him, my legs dangling off the side and his body pressed between them.

"The fact that you're even thinking about Jace tells me that I'm not doing a very good job of keeping your attention," he growls as he begins gently pulling my boots off and depositing them on the floor. My socks follow and then he reaches for the button of my jeans. His eyes meet mine in some sort of silent inquiry. I give the most imperceptible nod. He undoes my jeans and pulls them down my legs with my underwear. I bite my lip because right now, Adam Wellington looks like a Viking sex god as he pulls his shirt off and drags my ass to the edge of the table, placing each of my feet on the armrests of the chair.

"Would Jace do this?" he asks in a low gravelly voice as he leans in and runs his tongue up my slit. I'm propped up on my elbows watching him and it's the single sexiest moment of my life. He looks carnal like he would literally eat me. He grabs the vibrator and breaks open the package as he continues to stare at me.

"No," I whisper.

"Good answer because this," he says running the vibrator over the sensitive skin where his tongue was, "is all mine." And with that statement, his tongue joins alongside the vibrator as it inside me.

I let my head drop back onto the cold wood. A moment later, he pulls the vibrator away and unceremoniously drops it on the table.

"Fuck. Don't stop," I cry as his lips seal around my clit and his fingers thrust inside me.

He doesn't, he just doubles down on his efforts, dragging me one step closer to ecstasy with each lick of his tongue and slide of his fingers.

"God, I missed this," I whisper. He sucks harder on my bundle of nerves, and I detonate. I'm slightly aware of guttural noises leaving my throat but I have no control over that. My body trembles and writhes as I fall deeply into the abyss.

He's gentle as he finishes licking me. When I open my eyes, he pulls back and looks at me. He doesn't bother wiping my wetness from his beard and lips, and fuck, that's hot, like steamy-romance-book hot.

He stands and curses. He leans against the table as if trying to figure something out. "Hold on," he says. He walks quickly out of the room, and I'm left lying there with my legs spread open, feeling a little awkward that this man just gave me one of the best orgasms of my life and then quite literally ghosted me.

Just as I'm about to get upset, give up, and get dressed, he appears again holding...five condoms? What high-level sport does he think we're doing tonight?

I raise an eyebrow. "Better to be overprepared," he says as

he steps back between my legs and runs a finger up my slit. He pulls down his pants and places the condom on his erection.

He glides the head of his cock up and down over my folds, coating it in my juices. "Take your sweater off, beautiful. I want to see all of you," he commands. Now, normally, I don't want to be commanded, but for Adam...this time, I'll let it pass. I pull my sweater off and undo my bra, flinging it to the side. Adam's eyes darken as he runs his hand down my sternum, past my belly button, and to the top of my sex.

"You are so fucking beautiful, Isa," he coos as he lines up his cock with my entrance and slowly pushes inside, one delicious inch at a time.

He grins as he leans over me. "She was right about this table. It's the perfect height," he says.

I giggle and he groans. Then he starts moving and I groan. We find our pace, each thrusting in perfect rhythm as if our bodies were designed to be locked together in this way.

I feel myself getting closer to my climax. Adam lifts under my ass, aligning me with his cock, he quickens his pace. He's so wet from me that our bodies make gushing sounds that I might otherwise find embarrassing, but all my focus is on chasing my orgasm.

"Don't stop," I whimper.

"Give it to me, Isa. Come for me," he commands, and I don't know if it's his gruff voice, the way his cock slides against me in just the right way, or the way his hands grip my hips, but I go crashing into oblivion, crying out his name which echoes in the vastness of the room.

"Fuck!" he roars, following me with his own orgasm.

I'm vaguely aware of him losing control of his thrusts and then he stills, his erection jerking inside me. He leans over me and looks into my eyes before slowly, tenderly kissing me. I melt into the table.

This feels so good, so right. Yet, I feel like he's still holding back a little. Maybe he just needs more time. He's clearly not over his last girlfriend even after all these years. Or maybe it's just me...

"You're thinking too loud again," he mutters against my neck.

He tickles me and I laugh. He groans. "Careful, or we'll need condom number two now," he says as he pulls out and makes quick work of disposing of the condom.

"How's that ankle?" he asks when he comes back over. He picks it up and examines it.

"I'll live."

"Let's get you in the bathtub," he says.

"A bubble bath?" I ask with hope in my voice.

He chuckles. "Whatever the lady wishes."

"Well, right now, she's wishing for a bubble bath," I state as he pulls me up into his arms, leaving our clothes in the dining room as he carries me up to his bathroom. The dogs, as if sensing we want privacy, stay by the fireplace in the dining room. Or maybe we just scarred them for life? Not going to think about that.

CHAPTER NINETEEN

Adam

I wake to find Isa wrapped around me like ivy. My body feels on fire from the heat of her against me, but I don't want to move. I reach for my remote and turn on the ceiling fans in my room. Breathing a sigh of relief as the cool air circulates around us.

I run my hand down her back. Her skin feels like satin beneath my fingertips. She murmurs in her sleep and adjusts herself, nuzzling her face against my neck. Her knee is dangerously close to my dick, and I reach down to relocate it, so she doesn't wake to me writhing in pain.

Sunlight streams into my room. We slept in after our late night. I'm already hard again just thinking about it.

She stirs and her hand brushes against my erection. Her head pulls back and big sleepy eyes stare down at me.

"You have to be kidding me," she murmurs.

Shrugging, I smirk. "Morning wood," I state.

She rolls her eyes. "I think you have permanent wood."

I purse my lips as I ponder that, and she gives my chest a little shove. I grin at her. "Only around you, beautiful."

She giggles. And I smile, proud of myself for making her happy. Something inside me wants to make her happy all the time. I've wasted so much of our short time together being an ass. I need to change that.

"How's your ankle?" I ask as I reach down to examine it.

"It's fine. Just a little sore," she says as I gently lift her leg and look at the small bruise around her ankle. It doesn't look horrible, but it definitely limits what we can do today.

"We could take the horses back into town," I suggest.

She shakes her head. "Can I ask you something?" she says as she props her elbow on the bed and places her head in her hand. I follow suit so we're lying facing each other.

"Sure, but only if I can ask you something." I enjoy these question games we play.

"Fine. That's fair." She pauses.

"What?"

"The car thing...have you tried to get in one lately?"

I start to feel my defensive anger rise and I have to squash it down. "No. I gave up on trying that a long time ago."

"Did you stop riding in cars after..." She trails off.

"The accident?" I finish her sentence and she nods.

"If you don't want to talk about it..."

I reach over and brush my hand across her cheek. I don't ever talk about that night. But for reasons I don't understand, I want to tell her. "It was a long time ago. We were coming home from a late dinner party. A drunk driver swerved into our lane and hit us head-on. The car flipped and hit a tree. Everyone died...except me. I broke a leg and an arm and two ribs. I had a concussion and a bunch of cuts. I attended their funeral in a wheelchair." I pause, moving my memory to when I stopped riding in cars.

"I didn't have a reaction to cars at first. I was anxious

when I was in them, but then...after I got back from Paris, I witnessed a pretty bad accident in the city, and something about it...I just couldn't anymore. I would get these massive panic attacks. So, I stopped riding in cars altogether. I know, logically it's silly, but no matter how much therapy I've done, I haven't overcome it." I shrug.

"Thank you for sharing that with me," she says as she presses a hand to my chest. "Have you ever tried driving?"

I shake my head. "I got my license when I was sixteen and drove a little bit but then went off to college, and after that, I was just driven places."

Suddenly, she sits up and claps her hands. "Four-wheelers!"

"Sorry, what?" I ask.

"Max's brother, Winston, has four-wheelers. What if I got him to drop them off and we drove those into town? We could take the trail. No traffic," she suggests.

"I...don't know," I say, feeling my anxiety begin to uptick.

"How about just around the driveway first? For me... please?" she asks. Then she pauses. "I know that's a big ask. Sorry, sometimes I get overly excited about a new idea."

I pull her into my lap and kiss the tip of her nose. "It's alright. It's not a horrible idea. I don't know how I'd react. I don't think of a four-wheeler as a car, although they aren't super safe."

She rolls her eyes. "We'll wear helmets." She looks so hopeful, and something about that makes me want to try, which surprises me.

"Fine. Let's try it," I say.

She grins and leans forward, pressing her lips to mine. I roll us over so I'm on top. I press my erection against her center.

"How about we take care of that problem first?" she murmurs against my lips.

"It's a problem?"

She laughs as she grips my cock and I groan. "Sort of. But I have a solution," she says as she guides me toward her entrance. With my last ounce of restraint, I grab a condom and quickly roll it on before letting her go back to putting me where she needs me. We both let out deep breaths as I sink into her.

"Or...we could stay here all day," I suggest as I begin moving slowly, thrusting deeper with each stroke.

"Not a chance, you can't dick-notize me," she murmurs.

"Dick-notize?" I ask.

"You know, hypnotizing me with your dick," she explains.

I laugh. "Oh, beautiful, I think I like that."

"Me too," she breathes before I increase my pace and bring her to orgasm. When she screams my name, I decide that's my new favorite sound.

———

Bastian's eyes nearly double in size when Isa waltzes into my kitchen and announces that Max is bringing over four-wheelers.

"Say what?" he asks, his eyebrows shooting to his hairline.

"We're going into town," Isa declares as she wraps an arm around my middle and squeezes her body against mine. I admit, her body heat pressing into mine is comforting, but it in no way takes away my nerves. I feel as though my body is abuzz with anxiety.

"Wow...just...wow," he manages as he places a spoon down on the countertop.

He raises a quizzical eyebrow at me. I shrug. He smirks. I glare.

"OK, you two, enough with the silent conversation," Isa says as she looks between us. Then she focuses on Bastian. "I merely suggested that it's high time that Adam starts to work on his PTSD, and since he doesn't view four-wheelers in the same light as cars, I figured that was a great place to start."

"Right...start him on something way more dangerous... great plan," Bastian says, his voice laced with sarcasm.

Isa groans. "We're going to go slow. Just on the trail. No big deal. And seriously, after I flew off Cleo yesterday, it's probably safer than horses."

"Had I known you have a penchant for not staying on the horse, I would have packed a helmet and knee pads," Bastian retorts.

"That's enough, you two," I growl. "What's for breakfast?"

"Wow, good morning to you too, sunshine," Bastian says, batting his eyelashes.

I give him a pointed look. He sighs and points to the warmer. I open it and find two plates with quiche.

I take one out and set it at the kitchen bar. Isa and I eat in silence as Bastian drones on about the winter festival. Isa discusses it with excitement. Apparently, this is the big festival that Isa had mentioned to me.

A honk at the front of the house has me heading to the front door. I open it to find Max standing by a trailer with two four-wheelers on it.

"You ready for a joyride?" he asks.

"No," I state.

He laughs nervously. "Uh...Isa suggested..." He trails off as he motions to the four-wheelers.

"I know," I state flatly as Isa bounds out of the house behind me. Apparently, she woke our dogs who must have taken a nap after Bastian fed them breakfast. Because they come flying out the front door and run over to Max who laughs as he gets knocked to the ground and licked to death.

"Get off, you crazy mutts," he yells.

"Those are purebred rottweilers," I point out.

"And a Great Dane," Isa adds.

"Whatever...they need some mint mouthwash," he says as he gets onto the flatbed of his trailer and drives the four-wheelers down.

He parks them and hands us the keys, and then goes over all the safety information and how to drive them. We put on our helmets, and each get on one.

"You ready?" Isa asks.

I feel myself shaking a little, but this feels more like a bike than a car, or at least I keep telling myself that.

"Yeah...I'm ready," I say as I try driving it around the circular drive before I lead us down my driveway and onto the trail we took yesterday. Isa follows me. At first, I'm hesitant, but then something happens about halfway down the trail. The breeze blows against my face, and I breathe in the cold winter air, and suddenly...I feel free. I feel years of anxiety float away like clouds on a breezy day, parting to reveal the sun.

I go a little faster, and when we reach the park, I pull over. Isa pulls up next to me. I pull my helmet off and smile.

"I take it...you enjoyed that?" she asks cautiously.

"I did," I admit. "I enjoyed it a lot."

She smiles. "Good. Uh, should we just park them here? You think they'll be OK here?" she asks as she looks around us.

I turn off my ATV and pull the key out. "Isa, we're in Storyview Falls and it's the middle of winter. No one but us is coming here, and even if they did, I could probably park one of my cars here with the doors unlocked and nothing would happen."

She rolls her eyes and takes off her helmet. "Don't be so sure. Last spring, Eleanor Hudson, who owns the little gift shop next to Max's restaurant, left her car unlocked by acci-dent and Joey Lutz, this high school kid, decided to take it for a joyride. Fortunately, Sheriff Wallace caught him before he wrecked the thing. I think he's still grounded."

"Well, I guess I've missed out on all the town gossip," I say as we walk hand in hand to Main Street.

"Let's get ice cream!" Isa suggests.

"Ice cream? It's not exactly warm out," I laugh.

"It's not super cold. It's like what, forty-eight degrees? That's a winter heat wave around here," Isa protests as we come upon the small ice cream parlor that's a block down from the library.

She stops out front and I open the door with a shake of my head, motioning for her to enter. She walks inside like she owns the place. "Hey, Leo," she says warmly to an older gentleman behind the counter.

"Hey, shortcake, how are you?" he asks, walking around the glass cabinet filled with ice cream and hugging her. An irrational part of me wants to pry her from his embrace and tell him to lay off, but when I see his weathered hands as he pulls back and his white hair that comes out from under his baseball cap, I decide beating up an old man would be a bad idea.

"Who's your friend?" he asks as he looks over at me.

I hold out my hand to him. "Adam Wellington, sir. Nice to meet you."

His eyes widen a little, but he takes my hand and shakes it. "Nice to meet you too, Adam." He looks between us, and I can see curiosity sparking in his eyes. "What can I get you two?"

"The usual for me. And for Adam...what type of ice cream do you like? Or would you prefer a milkshake?" she asks me as she leans forward to look into the cabinet with the ice cream.

"Well, what do you recommend?" I ask as I step up beside her and begin to read the flavors.

"Isa here is a fan of my hot fudge sundae, which is pretty

darn good if I do say so myself. A lot of people like my peanut butter swirl in a waffle cone. And today's special is pistachio," Leo says.

I look at the menu on the wall behind him. "What's a torpedo deluxe?"

Isa giggles. "There's no way you can eat all of that. Only Phil Watts has managed to finish it."

"Phil?" I ask.

"He owns the insurance company on Preston Lane. And he got ten free cones because he finished it," Isa says.

Why do I feel like I know no one in this town? Once in a while, Bastian talks about people in town, but I never pay attention to their names.

As if reading my mind, Isa asks, "You really don't know people here, huh?"

I shrug. "I'll try it," I say to Leo.

Leo smiles. "Godspeed, kiddo. It's not for the faint of heart." He hands Isa a normal-sized sundae and then pulls out the largest bowl I've ever seen ice cream served in in my life and begins scooping various flavors into it.

"I tried to warn you," Isa says as she licks a spoonful of ice cream. Her eyes dance with humor as they meet mine.

Isa sits down at a small bistro table by the front window as I stand and watch Leo toss at least ten scoops of ice cream, a banana, hot fudge, caramel sauce, whipped cream, and a half dozen maraschino cherries into the enormous bowl. He brings it around the counter and sets it on the table. "If you can finish it in under forty-five minutes, you get ten cones free," he says as he holds out a spoon for me. "Good luck, kid."

I try a mint chocolate chip one first. "This is good," I muse.

"Leo makes all the flavors here. He's old school," Isa says in between bites. When she finishes, she sits back in her chair and watches me. "You really have never hung out in Storyview Falls, have you?"

"I did once upon a time. When I was little, we moved from the city here to live with my grandfather. But he insisted I attend the same boarding school he did and that starts in the fifth grade. So, I was only here for part of fourth grade. I vaguely remember getting ice cream here once or twice, but I never really got to hang out here," I explain.

"Well, you missed out," Isa says. She points out the window. "There's Kagan's Pharmacy, Elsa Palensky has a cute little gift shop she opened a few years ago; there's Heather Gordon's thrift store; Leslie Norman owns a pottery and art gallery at the end of the street, and you know Elisha. We could see what the movie theater is playing?" she suggests.

"Oh, I forgot there was one," I say as I keep shoveling ice cream into my mouth. The chime above the door rings as a customer enters.

"Hey, Leo," some young man says and glances over at us, his eyes widen. "Damn, you trying a torpedo?"

I nod and eat another bite. He leans out the window, "Hey, Aiden, check it out, some old guy is trying to eat a torpedo!"

I nearly choke on my ice cream. Isa starts silently laughing. "I'm not old," I mumble.

"You're ancient," she whispers with a smirk. I glare at her while trying to get halfway through the torpedo.

"Oh, shit, you think he can do it?" the kid, who I assume is Aiden, says.

"Language," Leo scolds.

"Leo, who was the last guy who ate one?" the other kid asks.

"Phil Watts," both Aiden and Isa answer.

"Right. That was like two years ago," the kid says.

"Zach, you gonna order ice cream or are you and Aiden just here to cheer on Mr. Wellington," Leo asks.

"Wait...as in *the* Mr. Wellington?" Zach asks.

"In the flesh," I say as an ice cream brain freeze starts.

"Slow down, mister, or you're gonna get brain freeze," Aiden suggests.

I rub my forehead and then go back to eating. Three more teenagers come in and soon a whole crowd is watching me.

I look at the clock on the wall. I have ten minutes left to finish this thing.

"You gonna make it?" Isa asks.

I look at what is seemingly a normal-sized sundae left in the long bowl. I nod. I'm committed now.

I start devouring it, bite by bite. The kids cheer as I swallow the very last puddle of ice cream in the bowl.

Leo rings a bell over the cash register. "We have a winner, folks!" He comes around with an old Polaroid camera, takes my photo with the empty bowl, and presents me with a certificate for 10 free ice cream cones. "Isa's sundae is on the house too. Hope to see you again soon, kid," Leo says before helping some other customers.

The teenagers are chanting, "Wellington. Wellington. Wellington."

"Wow, thirty minutes here and you've become a town hero," Isa teases.

I hold my belly. "I'm not feeling like one," I announce.

Isa bites her lip. "Sorry...you may be going into a sugar and lactose coma. We should probably get you something to soak it up," she muses.

"I don't think I can eat for another day," I state.

She pauses, purses her lips, and then smiles. "I have an idea."

"Thanks, Leo," she calls out as she grabs my hand.

This ought to be good.

CHAPTER TWENTY

Isa

I open the door to Main Street Arcade and Indoor Golf. It's a fun new property housed in an old department store building. Three floors of games and indoor golf.

"Wow. When did this place open?" Adam asks.

I smile. "Two years ago. I've only been a few times when Elisha drags me out. They have a bar up by the indoor golf area."

Adam looks mildly impressed as I lead him up two escalators to the top floor. The lights are dimmed up here and everything is lit up by black lights and glow-in-the-dark paint.

Adam places a credit card down. "My treat," he says with a smile.

"If you insist," I reply.

We grab putters and balls and head to hole number one.

"I have to warn you, I play golf," Adam says.

I roll my eyes. "I have to warn you, I spent summers

working part-time at one of the mini-golf places down by the beach," I reply.

"Well, then, shall we wager?" he asks, raising a suggestive eyebrow.

I laugh and shake my head. "Get your mind out of the gutter, Mr. Wellington," I tease.

"I don't think I will. I win, you spend the next two nights with me," he says.

"And if I win?" I ask.

"Winner's choice."

I cock my head to the side as I think about it. "If I win, you get to help me at the winter festival in two weeks."

"When is it?" he asks.

"It's on Saturday. Don't worry, it won't interfere with that busy work schedule of yours."

He looks a little hurt by my statement and I immediately want to take it back. But instead of responding, he just motions for me to putt.

"Ladies first," he says.

I line up my ball and send it sailing toward the hole. It gets an inch from its destination and stops.

"Ugh," I mumble as I knock it into the hole.

Adam steps up and gets a hole in one. He smirks and I groan.

"I should know by now that you're competitive. I just didn't realize you had any sporting skills," he states as we walk to the second hole.

"There's a lot you don't know about me," I reply.

"OK, let's go with a question per hole," he suggests. I grin. This question game is becoming our thing. And I love it.

"I like that," I agree as I look back at hole one. "What's the question for hole one?"

"Favorite food," he says.

I roll my eyes. "Cheese ravioli. What about you?"

"Not beef Wellington?" he replies with a wink.

I groan and give his giant bicep a little punch. "Very funny," I say dryly. "You didn't answer the question."

"I like street tacos."

"Really?" I ask.

"Yes. Really. There's this place a block from the helipad in the city. It's right by the subway and sometimes I stop and get them. They are definitely the best tacos I've ever had."

"OK. What's our question for hole number two?" I ask.

"You pick."

I contemplate. "How about...the happiest memory you have? Or something you want to accomplish?"

He grows silent and I wonder if I've overstepped with my questions.

"I'll answer both. I want to save my corporation from being taken over by James Titan. I have some plans, and hopefully, it works out. And my happiest memory...I was ten. We had just moved here to live with my grandfather. He wasn't doing great, but it was his birthday and he announced at breakfast that he wanted to go to the beach. My dad packed up our car, and with no particular plan, we just left and drove over to Triton Cove Beach. We parked in the public parking lot. We hauled our stuff down to the crowded beach. At some point, my dad went and got us sandwiches to eat on a picnic blanket. We built sandcastles and I took my boogieboard out into the surf. My grandfather taught me how to use it properly. It was a perfect, spontaneous day. He died before his next birthday when I was at boarding school. That was the last fun day I had with him. It was the only time we ever did anything like that."

"Mister, are you guys going to go?" a kid says from behind us.

"Play on through," Adam says to the three middle-school-aged kids.

"What about you?"

"I would love to buy that old property over on Crestwood and turn it into the town library. But that's a pipe dream. My happiest memory is Paris. I always wanted to see the Eiffel Tower. We didn't have a ton of money when I was a kid, but then when my dad's invention started to sell, we were able to take a vacation. My parents didn't tell me where we were going. They made me get a passport and said it was just good to have one since I would be an adult soon. And then a few months later, they took me to the airport, and at the check-in counter, I learned we were going to Paris." I smile at the memory. "I didn't sleep the entire way there; I was so excited. And then, when we arrived, Dad asked our taxi driver to take us by the Eiffel Tower on the way to our hotel. I remember stepping out of the car and just standing there, staring at it in total awe. It was a lifelong dream come true and it was a million times better than I could have imagined." I finish and Adam is staring at me with a goofy grin on his face.

"What?" I ask, wiping my lips wondering if I have ice cream on my face.

"Nothing. You're adorable, you know that?"

I blush. "I like that both of our happiest memories are with your families," I say as I line up my ball and hit it. This time I get a hole in one and he misses and needs the second shot.

"What's your worst memory?" I ask as we walk up to hole three. The words are out of my mouth before I can retract them. My hand flies to cover my lips. "Oh my God! I'm so sorry," I murmur from behind my fingers.

He reaches out and pulls my hand away, bringing it to his lips and kissing the backside. "You don't have to be sorry," he says as his eyes search mine. "Yeah, that day was definitely the worst, but honestly, I don't remember much of it. Finding Stephanie in bed with Jace...that was probably worse because

I remember every single image and sound from that moment," he says.

I tilt my head to the side, my curiosity getting the better of me. "So, Jace is bi?" I bite my lip. "Sorry, is that an inappropriate question?"

He shakes his head. "It's fine. And yes, he is, thus being with both Bastian and Stephanie."

"I'm sorry that happened to you, and to Bastian," I say. It's still weird to think of Jace as a bad guy when he's always been so nice to me.

"What about you?" he asks.

"Mine's silly. It doesn't matter," I mumble as I step up and place my ball on the green mat.

He steps behind me and wraps an arm around my waist, brushing a kiss to the back of my head. "Nothing that caused you pain is silly, Isa."

I take a deep breath and turn around. "My dog died." I pause and he looks confused. "I had a dog before Felipe. Barkley. Anyhow, he was a Great Dane also and he got something called bloat and we didn't catch it in time, and he died," I say quickly to keep myself from tearing up, the words coming out rushed and fused together.

"I'm sorry."

I shrug. "I had just graduated from college. He was my first dog. I had always wanted one but we didn't have a lot of money when I was little and then my parents didn't have the time and I was going to go off to college, so I waited and rescued Barkley from a Great Dane rescue. He was such a good dog."

Adam steps away and I hit my ball. This time we both get holes in one.

"Favorite song," Adam says as we step up to the fourth hole.

"Wow, way to try to lighten the mood. What if I say some really sad ballad?" I ask with a smile.

He laughs. "I was hoping for some goth heavy metal."

I giggle and he leans forward and kisses me. I suddenly wish we were back at his place...alone.

"Ewww. Grownups are so disgusting," some kid whispers as he walks behind me.

I laugh against Adam's lips and pull back. He's laughing too as we both just stare at each other. I don't know what it is about this moment with this man, but I feel a connection so strong it almost knocks the wind out of me.

His jaw clenches and I wonder if he feels it too. "Come on, let's finish this game so I can win," he teases. A small part of me wants to lose so I can spend the next two days at his place.

———

"I can't believe you won," Adam grumbles as we walk back to the four-wheelers.

"Oh, come on, don't be a spoilsport. That last shot was fair and square, and besides, I won us a free round of golf by hitting that impossible shot," I state as I reach for the helmet that I left on my four-wheeler.

"Fine, but next time don't expect me to go so easy on you," he murmurs. I giggle and then start back to his house. I watch Adam enjoy the ride and I hope it's building confidence in him to one day soon try getting in a car. But I decide to take it slow with him and not try to press him too much.

When we pull into his driveway and park the four-wheelers, he walks over and embraces me. "I know I lost the game but stay anyhow. Stay with me for another night...please?" he asks as he takes my cold face in his warm hands and presses his lips to mine. He's so warm and smells of pine and mint and something that's uniquely him.

"OK," I manage as he pulls back. "But I do have to go to the library tomorrow," I say.

"I'll get Bastian to take you."

I look down at my clothes. "Uh, I don't have a change of clothes," I state.

He pulls out his phone and opens some shopping app and hands it to me. "Buy anything you need. They'll deliver it by tonight," he says.

I give him a look that says he's being ridiculous. His stern stare tells me that he means business. I'm slowly figuring out his facial expressions, the tone of his voice, and even the ways he moves when he's calm or angry. I order a few things and hand him back his phone.

"You do know money doesn't solve every problem, right?" I ask him as we walk inside.

"I know that. But it solves a lot of them," he replies as our dogs come bounding toward us. I smile. Felipe has made friends and the way Isaac and Ames have accepted him as one of their pack warms my heart.

"Hi, buddy," I say as I pet him and then scratch Isaac's and Ames's heads.

"Did you two have fun?" Mrs. Potter asks as she rounds the corner from the back hall.

"We did. It was a fun day," Adam declares. "Can you ask Bastian to pretty please make us cheese ravioli and salad for dinner?" So much for not requesting particular meals from Bastian. That's two days in a row.

I blush when he turns and winks at me. How am I falling for him? I just met him. Yet...there's just something about him.

"Of course. Bastian made a minestrone and it's on the

stove whenever you want lunch or if you ate in town, I can have him put it in containers," she says.

"Oh, we'll try it. It sounds good," I say, feeling bad he went through the trouble.

I begin to walk toward the kitchen, but Adam sweeps me up and tosses me over his shoulder. I squeal.

Mrs. Potter laughs.

"We'll have it with dinner. I have to show Isa some things upstairs," he says as he carries me to his room.

"Adam!" I shriek as I giggle. I look down at Mrs. Potter from the landing at the top of the stairs. She's smiling at me, and I know I must be bright red.

When we get to Adam's room, he sets me down gently and takes my face in his hands. "I needed you to myself," he says as his thumbs trace my jawline.

"Adam," I start, but stop when I see the sincerity in his eyes.

"How?" he asks.

I frown. "How...what?" I ask.

He shakes his head. "Nothing."

I lean up and plant a kiss on his lips. "I think I know because I feel it too. And I don't know how we're connecting like this so quickly. It's like..."

"Magic? I thought we'd already established that," he finishes my thought.

I nod as he leans down and kisses me, this time our lips and tongues caress and lick and I get lost in him...in us.

"You know what else is magical?" he asks as he pulls back.

"What?"

He thrusts his hardness against me, and I laugh. "You're such a man-child," I tease.

"I'll show you that I'm much more man than child," he promises as he pulls my sweater over my head. And I decide

I'd like that...very much indeed. In fact, I'm beginning to like everything about Adam, and that is a little scary.

CHAPTER TWENTY-ONE

Adam

It's been two weeks. Two weeks of riding four-wheelers, going for walks in the snow, movie nights, and late nights in my bed. I've asked her hundreds of questions, and she's asked me even more. She's invaded my thoughts from the time I get up till the time I go to bed. I don't want to admit I'm addicted to Isa Garren, but I'm finding it hard to deny it with each passing day.

My phone pings with a text.

Isa: What's Bastian making for dinner? Or should I pick something up?

She's been trying to find ways to drive herself over here, but there's not a chance I'm allowing that. I prefer Bastian drive her. I didn't send his ass to a specialized defensive driving school for nothing. And besides, Isa's car is a death trap. I've already researched a car I want to buy her, one that has had zero fatalities.

Me: I'll have Bastian pick up food and you and Felipe.

Isa: What time?

Me: When do you finish work?

Isa: Library closes at eight tonight.

Me: 8:01

Isa: (eye-rolling emoji)

Me: If you keep irritating me, I'll come over there now and work from your desk.

Isa: Good luck finding space.

Me: Oh, beautiful, I will find space. Don't tempt me.

Isa: You're impossible.

Me: That's why you like me.

Isa: Nope, that's definitely not why.

Me: See you tonight.

Isa: Yeppers.

I smile. God, this woman is amazing. I sit doing my work while periodically remembering how Isa's body felt beneath me last night. After a day of mental distractions, I send Bastian a message to go pick up Isa and dinner.

Bastian: You are so bossy!

Me: I'm literally your boss.

Bastian: Whatever.

Me: Whatever doesn't sound like something a person who wants a pay raise says.

Bastian: WHATEVER

Me: You're a dick.

Bastian: "You're a dick" doesn't sound like something a boss would say.

Me: Go. Get. Isa.

Bastian: Fine!

I finish reviewing the contract on the property I'm considering buying in Storyview Falls and hit send on my email to my attorney to proceed with the purchase. When Isa told me about her dream property, my neurons began to fire. Just maybe, I might have a solution.

I tap my pen against my desk and look at the clock. It's been twenty minutes since Bastian left. They should be back by now.

I pull out my phone and text Isa.

Me: You running late?

No reply. No three dots. Nothing.

I text Bastian.

Me: What's your ETA?

No reply. I call him. He doesn't answer. I call Isa. She doesn't answer.

I call Mrs. Potter on the intercom.

"Yes, dear?" she answers.

"Have you heard from Bastian?"

"No." I can practically hear the frown in her voice. "Why?"

"He won't answer his phone and Isa won't pick up either."

"I'm sure they're fine. Maybe Felipe got out or something," she says but her voice indicates she's as worried as I am.

"I'm going to see," I state.

"Shall I have Thomas get Apollo ready?" she asks.

"No."

"You taking the four-wheeler?"

"No. I'm taking the car. It'll be faster," I announce.

Her gasp is audible and it's the last thing I hear as I hang up and go to the garage. Shaking, I find the key to my SUV and turn it on.

"You can do this," I say to myself.

"It's just a car and it's not even a full five miles," I remind myself aloud as if a pep talk is going to work.

I slowly pull out of the garage and turn onto the drive leading out to the road. As soon as I get away from the house, I realize I forgot my headlights.

"Stupid idiot," I chastise myself as I turn them on and make my way to the main road.

There aren't any other cars this late in the evening. Everyone is probably home for the night.

I head toward the town center. About a half mile from the library, I see flashing lights. And then I see two cars and one of them is mine. I immediately pull over. My knuckles are so white from gripping the steering wheel I'm surprised they haven't left marks on it.

I slowly open my car door and walk toward the police car. Flashes of memories from the accident that took my parents come crashing back to me. And then I see them.

Bastian. Isabelle.

Relief as I've never felt before floods my entire body.

Isa's talking to someone.

"Thanks, Sheriff Wallace. I'm just glad no one was hurt," she says before her eyes track to me.

A myriad of emotions run across those facial features that I've memorized in the one month since we met. She takes five long steps and wraps her arms around my waist.

I don't move for a minute but then I'm tugging her closer, burying my nose in her hair, kissing the top of her head.

"You're OK," I state more than ask.

"Yes, yes. We're fine. It was just a fender bender. You need a new rear bumper. Jake McCreary lost control on a patch of ice. It's fine," she says soothingly. "You drove?" she asks against my chest.

"I did," I say, still a bit in shock that I did that.

I look around for this Jake McCreary man that I'm most definitely going to pummel, but aside from the small cluster of townspeople on the sidewalk, the only other person there is a kid who can't be more than eighteen.

He looks terrified.

Isa pulls back as Bastian steps over to me. "How..." He

starts but trails off as his eyes find my SUV. "You drove?" he asks.

I swallow and nod.

"Shit. You drove," he says his serious demeanor switching to one of exuberance. He grabs my shoulders over Isa's head and gives them a little shake. "C'est incroyable!" he yells with a giant grin on his face, but his excitement fades as he sees my pained expression.

"Adam, this is good, no?" he asks in confusion.

"I thought..." I trail off unable to speak my worst fears.

"Oh, merde," he replies. "I'm sorry. I was talking to the sheriff and poor Jake was a mess. We were just wrapping up here. So, we can all head home now. Do you want me to drive you back?"

I take a deep breath and look over at my other car. Bastian has it pulled into a street parking spot.

"No," I say, my voice low and vibrating with nerves. "I'll drive us all back in my car. Tomorrow we can call to have that one towed for repair."

Jake comes over to us and I stare down at the pimple-faced teenager who looks on the verge of tears. "I'm so sorry, Mr. Wellington. I didn't see the black ice, I swear. I'm so sorry," he says. I look over and see his car has a lot more damage.

I want to scream at him that he could have killed the two people I love most. Love? Yes, I love them. Shit, I love Isa. Fuck! This is not the time to have that epiphany. But I look down at Isa and I know I can't be that person, not right now.

"Have Jake's car towed as well. It's not your fault, kid, but if I ever hear of you being reckless with your driving, so help me..." I trail off as I glare at him.

"Th-thank y-ou, Mr. Wellington, s-sir," Jake stammers. I don't give him a chance to say more as I lead Isa back toward my SUV. I open the back seat for her, realizing as I'm helping her buckle in that it's the same seat I was sitting in on the day of the accident, right behind the driver. That seat saved my life.

Bastian gets in the passenger seat, and I open the driver's door and stare inside for a long moment, feeling the adrenaline leaving my body.

I clear my throat and take a seat, closing the door and turning on the car. I drive home even more cautiously than I had driven there. As I pull into the driveway, I realize Felipe isn't with us.

"Felipe?" I ask.

"Elisha is watching him tonight. He didn't finish his dinner yet, so she said she'd check in on him and again in the morning before she opens the café," Isa explains as I park the car.

"I see," I say. I get out of the car in a bit of a trance and walk into my home where I promptly pour a double of scotch and toss it back in a single swallow, letting the amber-colored liquid burn my throat as it slides down.

I feel Isa's arms wrap around me and she presses her face against my back. "I'm so proud of you," she says softly.

I put my glass down and turn to face her, looking her up and down again for injury, but she's fine.

"I swear. I'm perfectly fine. He didn't even hit us hard. It was like bumper cars at an amusement park," she swears.

I let out a shaky breath. "You scared me to death. I..." I trail off, lost for words.

"I'm sorry. I'm so sorry I didn't think to call you right away, so you wouldn't be worried. Sheriff Wallace was right there and then once we figured out it was mostly just the fenders and Jake's front grill, I just figured it wouldn't take long to get a police report and exchange insurance information," she assures me, but nothing about it feels reassuring.

I'm about to tell her that when Mrs. Potter throws open the door and walks over to Isa.

"Are you alright? Bastian said you were alright, but I had to check with my own two eyes. You poor dears. And you, I can't believe you drove. I'm..." She bursts into tears, and I stifle a groan. Great, just what I need, a weepy Mrs. Potter.

Isa hugs her.

"We're both fine. It was such a minor thing. I promise," Isa says.

Mrs. Potter pulls away and wipes her eyes with her apron. "I know. We should be so thankful it was just a little minor incident. Well, you two enjoy your evening," she says. She turns at the door. "You're going to the annual board dinner tomorrow night, yes?"

I nod. "We'll take the helicopter," I state, deciding my one car voyage is my final one.

"Oh, alright, then. I'll make sure the pilot is on standby. Bastian has the food waiting for you," she says.

"Head on home, Mrs. Potter. I'll clean up after us," I state as I continue looking at Isa.

"Oh...uh, if you insist," she says.

"I insist."

"Well, I'll let Bastian know. Goodnight," she says as she leaves us alone.

"I want to check on Bastian. Meet me in the dining room?" I ask Isa.

She bites her lip and gives me a tentative nod. I feel like she wants to say something and is holding back, but right now, I need to make sure my best friend is alright.

I find him putting on his jacket.

"Food is out. Mrs. Potter said *you* are cleaning up?" he asks with a raised eyebrow.

I embrace him and he goes stiff as a board.

"I'm glad you are OK," I state as I pat his back and pull away.

"Well, that was weird. And yes, I'm fine. What the hell is wrong with you?" he asks.

"I...I'm fine," I lie.

"Right. You're great. You drove for the first time in a decade. You came upon an accident scene with people you care about. And now you want to clean. Sure, yeah. Totally normal," he muses .

"Fuck off. I'm fine," I mutter.

"And there he is," Bastian says with a smile as he pats the top of my head like a small child.

I brush his arm away. "You're really fucking the worst, you know that?"

"Right back at you. I'll see you in the morning, my little speed racer," he says with a wink as he exits the kitchen.

I walk into the dining room and find Isa sitting and staring at her plate. It's takeout from Max's restaurant. We eat in silence. I catch Isa looking over at me on three different occasions. I know what I need to do but she's going to fight me on it, that I know for sure.

I clear our plates and put them in the dishwasher with Isa's help, and when we finish, I lead her to my room. I strip off her clothes slowly and then mine. I lay her on my bed and make love to her. This time feels different, I feel a connection that I've never felt before. It feels more intense, more real, and that scares the shit out of me.

As we're lying there afterward, Isa's head on my chest, her body tucked against mine, I look down at her. "No more cars," I declare.

"Adam, be serious," Isa says with a sigh.

"I am. No more cars. I'll get you a four-wheeler and you can take it on the path," I state.

She raises her head. "We've already discussed that those are actually more dangerous than a car."

"Doesn't matter," I say.

"Oh, for the love of..." She trails off. "I have my own car, you know. You can't stop me from driving it."

"That death trap? Hell yeah, I can. That thing is going straight to the dump once I find it," I state.

"Adam, you're being totally unreasonable."

I take her face in my hands as I roll us so that I'm hovering over her. "You are the most precious thing in my life, Isa. I'm not going to lose you."

Her hand touches my cheek. "Oh, Adam. You won't lose me. I'm right here. And I'm fine. And besides, you can't lock me away in a tower and stop me from living. I need my independence. I need my car. That's non-negotiable."

"You could have...I can't live like that."

"Let's get some sleep. Things will be better in the morning," she says as she pulls my head down to her breasts. I kiss each one and then roll us back over. She curls up against me and falls asleep. I lie awake for hours, listening to her soft snores. I vow at that moment that I will protect her, even if that means protecting her from me and my messed-up mind.

CHAPTER TWENTY-TWO

Isa

Yeah, sleeping on it did not make it better. By breakfast, Adam has doubled down.

He sips his coffee slowly while staring at me. "I'm serious, Isa," he says as he places it down on the counter. I can see Mrs. Potter and Bastian both look over at us and then quickly look away.

"About what?" I ask innocently hoping this is about something else but knowing damn well it's not.

"No more cars," he states emphatically.

I roll my eyes. "Fine. Let's just say we never drive or ride in a car again. Then what?" I ask, playing devil's advocate because this man is being completely irrational. I understand partly why he is this way, but he had come so far. I mean, he freaking drove a car yesterday!

"What do you mean? You can use the ATVs, the horses, the helicopter, subways, and boats, but no cars."

"Great. So, none of those things can have accidents,

then?" I pause and then glare. "Oh, wait. I just got thrown off the horse a few days ago. And did I ever tell you about my friend whose dad was in the Navy and died in a helicopter crash? Oh, and my other friend's brother is in the Coast Guard, and he has to respond to boat accidents all the time." I put my hands on my hips as if that gesture is going to make my point seem more persuasive.

"I don't care. I've seen enough with cars to know I can't ride in them or have the ones I love riding in them," he says.

I point to Mrs. Potter and Bastian. "So, none of us can drive or ride in cars anymore?"

Bastian's eyes are wide. "Fuck no. Don't bring me into this," he says with a wave of his hand.

"Well, he loves you too, whether he wants to admit it or not," I state.

"Well, Bastian's car is not a death trap," Adam says.

"Oh, so if I get a new car, then it's fine," I retort with a groan. This man is killing me!

"No. You can't ride in any car. I...just no, Isa," he replies with a look of panic in his eyes. He's being completely irrational still. Wonderful.

"Adam, I can't live like that. I'm sorry, but I need to drive, and I need to be able to ride in cars. I understand your fear, I do. I'm so proud of you for driving last night. But fender benders happen. Hell, I backed my car into a sign a few years ago and it still has a dent. It's not a big deal. I was protected because I was in the car," I say, trying to persuade him when I know that's an impossible task.

"Please..." He trails off as he steps toward me with pleading eyes.

"I'm sorry, but no," I state.

He swallows. "I'll be back," he says as he walks out of the kitchen.

I turn to Mrs. Potter and Bastian. "Was he like this...

before?" I ask, swallowing my nerves and the sinking feeling I have that Adam and I just reached an impassable point in our relationship.

Bastian shrugs, but Mrs. Potter slowly nods. "This...he was never this unreasonable, Isa. He never dictated what others could do. I'm sorry. He must care for you very much," she says with a sad smile.

"I can't *not* drive," I state.

"Merde. He was doing so well. I thought...maybe..." Bastian trails off as he looks at the doorway. Adam is standing there with a pile of books. He takes ten giant steps and sets them on the counter. "I'm releasing you from our agreement, Isa. You can have the books. They are yours...or the library's. Whatever you wish to do with them, do it. I...can't be the man you need me to be, and you deserve more." He reaches out and brushes a hand over my cheek. I feel tears welling in my eyes.

I slap his hand away. "You're just giving up, already. That's it. One small thing and you're out?" I go from sadness to anger in less than three seconds, because of the audacity of this man. "You know what. Screw you, Adam. You're right. I do deserve better. And the worst part of this is you are being totally irrational, and you absolutely can give me more. But if this is how you deal with one little car accident and a fight over driving, then...fine. Live your lonely-ass life here in your fucking palace. I hope you're very happy...by yourself!" I yell, my voice getting a little louder with each word.

I spin on my heels. "Goodbye, Mrs. Potter. Goodbye, Bastian," I say as I dart out of the room. I make it to the front hall when Bastian comes running after me with the pile of books.

"The books," he says.

"Why?" I say loudly.

"Isa, let me take you home. I'll leave early. Come on," he offers as he steps toward me.

I swallow a wash of sadness and nod while I blink back tears. He walks out front and presses the unlock button on his car fob. I get into the passenger seat. He pulls out a box from the back of his car and sets the books inside it, placing it on the back seat.

Neither of us speaks as he drives me home. When we reach my apartment, he turns to me.

"Don't give up on him. Please," he begs.

"I can't. I'm sorry, Bastian, but maybe he's right. If he can't get past whatever his issue is, then I'm not sure there's a future for us, no matter how I feel about him," I state.

"Just...give him some time. He's been through a lot," he explains.

"I know, but it's not an excuse," I argue.

"It's not, but it is an explanation." He pauses and looks into my eyes. "I know he can be a jerk. I know he can be an overbearing, grumpy, alphahole. I know he can be difficult."

"Wow, you're really good at selling your friend," I say dryly.

"*But* he's the best man I've ever met. If he were gay, I would totally be with him. He's a better friend than anyone in my life and he loves hard, maybe too hard. I promise you, his irrational behavior is coming from a place of love for you. He'll come around. I know he will," Bastian argues.

"Bastian..." I trail off with a sigh. I'm too tired to argue. I feel like the weight of the world is on my shoulders. "I'll see you later," I state as I get out of the car.

"Don't forget the books," he adds.

Cursing Adam, I reach into the back seat and take the box of twenty-eight priceless books. It seems unceremonious to carry them inside in a brown cardboard box, but I'm not giving up on my dreams, and if Adam's parting gift is the equivalent of several million in books, then so be it.

I shut the door and head inside Elisha's café. I don't want to go home. I need my best friend.

When she sees me, she pauses cleaning the counter, and steps around it. She says nothing as she walks across the open space, removes the box from my arms, and sets it down before enveloping me in a hug. And that's when I lose it. I've broken up with boyfriends before, boyfriends I've had longer than Adam, but this…this is unbearable. I feel like a piece of me has been ripped off and tossed away. It's hard to breathe.

"Take a deep breath," Elisha says.

I try, and instead, inhale too quickly. Hiccups start racking my chest.

"Sit down. I'll get you some tea," she says as she pulls out a chair and forces me to sit in it.

I put my head in my hands. The bell over the door rings.

"What's wrong with Isa?" Ella's voice whispers from a few feet away.

"Oh, she met a douchebag and he just showed his true douchebag colors. What can I get you, Ella?" she asks.

"Just a black tea, please," Ella says. "Wait, is this…" She looks around and lowers her voice, "Adam Wellington?"

"Yep," Elisha answers for me.

"Damn. That sucks," she says.

"You working an extra shift again?" Elisha asks.

"Yep. Gotta pay the bills," Ella says with a tired groan.

"Well, that we can all relate to," Elisha replies.

Ella turns back to me. "Sorry, Isa. Men are…well, stick with us girls, we're better."

I sadly nod as I feel tears falling down my face. She reaches over the counter, grabs a few napkins, and hands them to me.

"Thanks," I whisper.

"What's with the box?" she asks.

I shrug. "First-edition books for the library. We're going to have a special exhibit soon, if I get this grant," I say but suddenly I'm not as excited. All the anticipation I had when I had left a month ago and gone to the Wellington Estate, all the excitement is gone.

"Hey, that's great news! This is the grant you needed a match for, yes?" Ella asks.

"This girl is gonna make the library so much better," Elisha encourages from behind the counter as she sets down Ella's tea and then comes around to set one in front of me.

"Now you're just being kind," I manage in between my dying hiccups.

"That's not true. Look at everything you've already accomplished. If Adam can't see how amazing you are, then he's the only person in this town who's blind to it," she says, her voice filled with grit. I want to argue that that's not the issue, but I'm too tired to argue with Elisha.

"What can we do to help?" Ella asks. I give her a sad smile. She's always so sweet and helpful. And I know she has it far worse than me.

"I'll survive. I'll just focus on the winter festival," I mutter as I reach for the tea.

"Oh crap, it's like in this weekend, right?" Ella questions.

"Damn straight. It's gonna be lit!" Elisha says enthusiastically.

I laugh and Ella tries to hide a giggle.

Two young girls at the corner table with their computers try to hide giggles.

"Oh, for the love of...can I seriously not say that? I give up!" Elisha states with hands on her hips. "I'm either too old to say things or I'm talking too old. Is there some not old but not young appropriate lingo for me?" she asks.

Ella smiles at her. "I say talk however you want." She gives me another brilliant Ella smile. "I'm serious about helping at the festival when I finish my morning cleaning. I hope...well, I hope you feel better," she adds.

"Thanks, Ella," I say quietly as she nods and heads out the door.

"Come on, I'll get you a cookie and then we are going to come up with a plan to get this grant," Elisha states as she motions to the box of priceless books. I know I should feel better with my best friend helping me, but deep down, I just want Adam to be here, and that hurts more than not having my grant. But if I learned one thing from him, it's to persevere no matter what happens. And that lesson now feels bittersweet since I'm doing it despite him.

CHAPTER TWENTY-THREE

Adam

I stare at the screen. They can't be serious. I had the dwelling on the property inspected and it needs so much work, it's pointless trying to save it. And I had wanted to save it for so many reasons. That assessment had ruined my plans for it. Except now the owners won't sell unless I agree to a condition to preserve it, which will cost me substantial time and money. I pick up my phone and call Cruz.

"Before you start, I'm just the bearer of bad news. I tried twelve different ways to get them to agree to something else, but they won't budge," he states.

"Did you call the attorneys?"

"Yep."

I feel my jaw clenching. "Did you check with our—"

"Adam, I've tried it all. This isn't my first dog and pony show. We either commit to restore it and use it for...well, something, or we walk...and if we walk..." He trails off because I know he's afraid to say it.

"Titan wins. He gets the property and we lose our last hope to ward off his takeover," I state. I know Titan's figured out my move because he's been trying to get this property for the last week.

"Fuck it. Tell them..." I stop as I look down and see something sticking out from a pile of papers on my desk.

I pull it out. It's a book Isa was reading. A sad smile ghosts my lips. I look around my office. Ames and Isaac are curled up in the corner asleep. They've seemed as glum as me the past few days.

"Adam?" Cruz interrupts my thoughts.

"Give me a minute. I'll call you back," I state, hanging up. I stare down at the book.

A knock on the door peels my attention away from one of the last remaining reminders of Isa left in my house.

It's Mrs. Potter.

"Adam?" she says as she looks at the book in my hands.

"Yes?" I stare at her, this woman who is the last remnant of a motherly figure I have.

She crosses the room and stands at my side, placing a hand on my shoulder. "It's not too late," she says softly.

"For what?" I ask, looking up at her.

"For love, Adam. For love," she says as she squeezes my shoulder.

I shake my head. "No. She deserves better. I..." I trail off and try to center my thoughts. "She was right, Petunia. I was trying to control her because I'm in love with her and if something happened to her...I couldn't live with it." My admission shocks even me.

Mrs. Potter smiles. "I know you are, Adam. Love is scary. I know it's even scarier now. You loved two people with all your heart, and you couldn't protect them, and they left you. But, my sweet boy, you can't be scared of losing those around you. Because you know what's scarier than losing them?"

I shake my head.

"Never having felt their love at all," she says. "Think of all the goodness Isa has brought into your life these past few weeks. You've changed. You're happier. You're that little boy I met so many years ago. And I know it's been hard, losing your grandfather and then your parents, and of course, Stephanie, but don't give up on love, my sweet child. Embrace it. You can't push the ones you love away every time something scares you. Eventually, they won't come back. You need to fight for the ones you love. Fight for Isa. She's worth it...and so are you."

"I...what if...I'm broken," I manage.

"No, you're hurt. But you aren't broken. If you were broken, you'd have never felt love for Isa at all."

My eyes widen. Is she right? Could she be right?

"You can still have happiness, Adam. You just have to go get it," she says with another squeeze of my shoulder.

"But what if it's too late?" I muse as I consider her words.

"If you believe that, then you didn't learn anything from Isa. She didn't give up. She came knocking on your door," Mrs. Potter says with a smile.

My sad smile begins to morph into a genuine smile. She's right. Isa didn't give up, and neither should I.

I rise to my feet and wrap my arms around Mrs. Potter embracing her and lifting her off the ground. "You're right! You are so right, Mrs. Potter," I exclaim.

"Adam George Wellington! Put me down this instance!" she yelps, and I laugh as I gently set her down. I kiss her cheek, and she blushes and waves a hand at me.

"I have to go clean up the kitchen and make sure Bastian hasn't burned it down," she says as she scurries out of the room. I pick up the phone and call Cruz.

"I have an idea. Well, I had a flash of this idea before, but now, it's happening. Tell them we're doing a full restoration and I'm sending over details on what that means right now. Get that contractor we worked with on the project last spring to come look at the property tomorrow. I want to close today," I state.

"Oh. Uh, OK," Cruz says, lost for words which is a first.

I hang up and make a half dozen other calls. If I can pull this off, then just maybe…maybe Isa will forgive me.

———

I walk through the house. I've had three crews working here in round-the-clock shifts for nearly two weeks. I didn't think it would be possible, but nothing good was ever easy. But this house…makes it look like it was easy.

"There are a few little things upstairs in the office spaces that need to be completed. But otherwise…I think it's ready," Cruz says as we stare at what I hope is going to be the new home for the Storyview Falls Library. That is if Isa agrees to it.

I've spent every waking moment making sure this place is perfect. The house was an enormous building. Nearly five thousand square feet including the attic, which I've turned into a private office just for Isa. God, I hope this works.

It's pained me to keep my distance from her. I did try once to text her, but she didn't reply to my text. I inquired with Bastian who asked Elisha and Elisha basically said I should go fuck myself. So that went well.

But then I showed up in person. I got chewed out by Elisha for about thirty minutes straight and then she finally let me talk. And when I finished, she was wiping tears away. I hope that's a good sign. Apparently, whatever I said made her switch to…what did she call it… Team Adam because after that she's been trying to plant a seed with Isa that maybe I'm not a lost cause. Even Max and Bastian have been attempting to help me. They all know about my plan...my grand gesture or at least that's what Bastian and Max deemed it.

But my biggest breakthrough was driving over here every day for the past ten days. It's been hard some days, but I keep trying. Bastian made me go back to therapy, which I had stopped for a while, and I hate that he was right. I needed it.

"If this doesn't work, then you have no chance," Bastian's voice comes from behind me.

I turn and give him the middle finger. "Is everything else set?" I ask.

"Oh yeah. Elisha, Ella, and Max are all down at the festival helping her set up. It's going to be epic!" Bastian assures me.

"Let's hope so," I say.

"I mean...way to not half-ass this apology," he says with a laugh.

"Whatever. I should probably head over there. I think this is as much as we'll have done for today," I state.

Bastian rolls his eyes. "Seriously? You've basically rebuilt this catastrophe of a building in under two weeks. It's wired for state-of-the-art technology. It has two floors of shelves, meeting spaces, an audio/visual space, a special exhibit hall, and offices for staff. Plus, the security features are sick as fuck. Like seriously, if she doesn't like it, I'm going to question her sanity," he says.

"She's headstrong. What if..." I trail off not wanting to finish the thought.

"It's enough. You are enough. Jesus, I thought we were making progress here," he groans.

I sigh and run a hand over my trimmed beard. "We are. *I* am," I state.

"Good. Then fucking act like it. Let's roll," he says as he motions for me to leave the house.

"Did the—"

"It's fine! Let it go!" Bastian yells from behind me as I step through the door's threshold.

He claps me on the back. "You go this. Go get your woman."

My woman. God, I hope this works and I can say that she is in fact mine by the end of the day.

CHAPTER TWENTY-FOUR

Isa

"Thanks again, Ella. You've been a big help," I state as I hurry to straighten the books on my display.

"Congrats, by the way," she says, motioning to the sign I have hanging in the background of my kiosk. I got the grant application submitted on the last day and I just found out yesterday that we got it. I cried when I opened the email. I cried more when my parents told me how proud they were of me. Speak of the devils.

"Hey, turtle dove!" my father says as he walks over with my mom.

"Hi, Dad. Hi, Mom," I say as I hug them both.

"It looks great! Job well done!" Dad says as he takes it all in.

"You really outdid yourself this year," Mom adds as she examines my grant poster.

"Well, we have reasons to celebrate, right?" I say as I lean my head on my dad's shoulder. They know a little about my time with Adam, but I played it off as no big deal. They don't need to know that my heart is broken.

He wraps an arm around me. "Yes, we do. Hey, did Mom tell you about the cruise we found for a month?"

I laugh. "You two and your cruises. I swear, you go from one to the next."

"You should join us sometime. They are a blast," Mom says.

"Hey, sorry to interrupt, but the band is setting up and wanted to know if they can start playing or if you wanted to say a few words first. The mayor is here, so..." Elisha says as she steps in front of me.

"Oh, right. Sure. Let's get this show on the road," I say as I step away from my father and fix my hair.

I walk over to the gazebo that sits just off Main Street by the park. Mayor Ginny Ashbury shakes my hand. "Great to see you, Isabelle. Congrats on that grant," she says.

I grin. "Thanks. It's really exciting."

The small crowd quiets as I step up to the microphone. "Thank you all for coming to our fifth annual Winter Book and Arts Festival. As most of you may have already heard, our library was awarded a prestigious grant yesterday and I just want to thank you all for continuing to be great patrons of our town's little library. We may be small, but we are mighty. I want to thank Mayor Ashbury for all her help in organizing today's festival. Mayor, would you like to say a few words?" I step back so she can take the microphone.

"Let's give our town librarian, Isabelle Garren, a round of applause," she says as she claps her hands and everyone else joins in.

I blush and nod at them.

"I have another surprise for you, Isabelle. I was contacted this week by someone who wanted to donate something to the library, something you've mentioned to me before, and I think you are going to like it, very much. I made him promise to wait until today to reveal it to you," she says with a wink.

I see him then. The crowd parts like he's an island in the middle of a river. But they don't need to part to make him stand out. His huge frame towers over most of them as he steps toward me.

I hardly notice when Mayor Ashbury pulls out a rendering of a building...a house...*the* house. It's the one I've always wanted to turn into the library. The old Bradley house on Crestview Drive. It's the last giant parcel of land that remains near the strip of buildings here. It's been for sale for a long time, but even with my grant, there was no way I could afford to purchase it.

Adam looks at me for a brief instance before shaking Mayor Ashbury's hand.

"I am pleased on behalf of the Wellington Foundation to present Ms. Garren with the keys to what I hope will be our town's new library," he says as he removes an old skeleton key from his pocket and holds it out to me.

I study it for a long beat before accepting it with a shaking hand. Our fingers touch and Adam looks into my eyes as if it's painful to be near me. I swallow and focus past him for a second, so I don't give in to the tears that threaten. I want to scream at him. I want to kiss him. Wait, do I want to kiss him? Still, after everything? He did try to text me, but I kept my gumption and didn't reply. My heart couldn't stand hurting again so soon.

Everyone is clapping and I smile and hold up the key after noticing the mayor giving me a look. I step up to the podium. "What a surprise. I'm excited to see what this property has to offer. The future of our town's library looks very bright indeed," I manage as the crowd cheers. I step back.

"Enjoy the day, everyone, and please don't forget to put in

for the raffles. They all go to support the library fund," the mayor adds as she closes the formal part of the day.

"Great job, Isa. It looks like we're going to have another successful winter festival," the mayor says. I nod and smile, thanking her before I swivel to face Adam. We're alone in the gazebo. It's a warm winter day, but still cold enough to require coats. He looks handsome in his black wool coat. He always looks handsome.

He swallows. "Can I...take you over to see the house?" he asks.

"Adam...I...I'm really busy. It's the festival," I state as I motion around us.

"I know...but I think your booth is under control," he says as he points. I look over to see Ella and Elisha waving at us. Wait a goddamn minute. Did they know?

I turn to ask him, but my parents step up by us.

"That's an amazing thing you did," my dad says as he holds out his hand. Adam shakes it.

"Thank you..." He trails off.

"Josh Garren," Dad says.

Adam's eyes widen. "Oh, you're Isa's father."

Dad nods. "This is my wife, Amanda Garren."

"Very nice to meet you both. I've heard great things about you from Isa...we've uh, recently become acquainted," he says.

"I've heard. It's great you were willing to give your collection to the library. Sounds like it really helped Isa land that grant," Dad says.

I look at Dad and smile but then he opens his mouth to speak again. "I sure hope Isa's relationship with you didn't unfairly give her the money," he says, his voice light-hearted as if he's teasing Adam.

I stare at him and then Adam in confusion.

"I assure you that the charity operating that grant has a strict protocol for grant approvals. I have nothing to do with it," Adam says as he quickly glances in my direction. What the fuck? No. No, no, no. Realization begins to slowly dawn on me as Adam continues. "We provide funding to that charity, but they also receive funding from a few other sources, so I can promise you my word means very little even if I had spoken up."

"Well, I'm just so proud of our daughter. She's doing amazing things with our little library," Dad says as he puts his arm around my shoulder and squeezes me.

"Thanks, Dad," I manage but my eyes stay locked with Adam's.

"Josh, come say hi to Mrs. Carwell. She's brought the most beautiful poinsettias and we need one," Mom says from behind us.

"Good job, turtle dove. I'll see you later," Dad says as he kisses the top of my head and goes to join Mom. He wraps an arm around her, and I look past them to see Ella visibly swooning over my parents' affection overload. I roll my eyes and then steal myself as I turn back to Adam.

"It's your charity?" I ask, my voice coming out like venom.

Adam's chest rises and then falls. "It's not *my* charity, Isa. But yes, my foundation does provide it quite a bit of support. You won the grant fair and square. I promise you I did not interfere."

I glare at him. "You know, you're unbelievable. Do you think throwing money at my pet project is going to undo what you did? Think again, Mr. Wellington," I say as I go to turn but his hand grabs my arm.

"Isa," he says, his voice low and pleading.

I spin on my nonexistent heels and point a finger at his chest and then quickly drop it as I remember we're in the middle of the winter festival and I don't need any prying eyes. "No. Not here. Not now. I have things to do today."

He slowly nods. "Will you...at least come to see the property later?"

I hate him. I hate that he's probably helped me win this grant. I hate that he bought my dream property for the library and gifted it to me. I hate that he's...doing all these nice things after he was such a controlling jerk.

He's swooped into my life...fine, I sort of knocked on his door, so maybe that's my fault, but then he had to be all charming and secretly really kind... argh!

I march back over to my booth and plaster on a fake smile as I begin greeting people. It takes all my willpower not to glance back over at Adam.

"Your parents are so cute. I wish I had that," Ella whispers as she hands me some flyers.

I groan. "They are irritating...but yes, they are cute." I look over at my parents who are walking arm in arm. For the briefest of moments, that little girl's desire to have what they have overcomes me. I swallow hard, trying to physically push back down that silly dream, a mere remnant from the days when I believed in fairy tales and princesses.

I try to find Adam in the crowd, but he's gone. I turn away from the people in my booth, pretending to grab more bookmarks from a box under a table. But really, I just need a second to steady my feelings. Because no matter how mad I am at him, I can't help that somehow deep down, I still love him.

———

I stick the last of the leftover handouts in a box and pack it into a little trolley I rolled over here from the library.

"I'll take it back," Ainsley says. I hug her. She showed up three hours ago to help.

"You didn't have to come back from your friend's house for this," I point out for the tenth time.

"Yes, I did. I never miss it," she says grinning. Then she gives me a little shake and giggles. "Aren't you excited? There's so much happening! It's all the stuff you used to talk about when I first started and it's really happening! It's like...a fairy tale!" she says, her face splitting as her smile widens.

I give her a small smile back. "It's great. I'm excited for the future of Storyview Falls Library."

She gives me a quizzical look. "And?"

"And...what?"

She rolls her eyes. But then pauses and her eyes widen as she stares at something behind me.

Adam is driving up to our booth. He parks a car; one I haven't seen before and gets out.

Then I see Jace, and I grimace. I give Adam a pleading look. I can't have this turn into some town spectacle.

"Hey, congrats on the new library. It sounds like you have a lot of amazing things happening here," Jace says. His back is to Adam, and he clearly has no idea Adam is walking this way.

"Oh, uh, yes! We do. Did you get a chance to check out our new exhibit?" I ask, referencing the first editions from Adam.

He nods. "I did. It's a great exhibit. I even learned a few things about Charlotte Bronte. Anyhow, I heard there was an opening on the library board."

Adam steps up beside him and I almost want to shield Jace.

"There is...are you interested in applying?" I ask. I have a small board of residents that meets monthly to discuss the library and the town's needs. They are all prominent members of the town, so it would be strange for Jace to be a member since he's not here often. Although I swear, I see him more than some people in town that hang out on Main Street daily.

"You should apply," Adam's deep voice penetrates the winter air.

Jace turns slowly, his eyes widening as he realizes who spoke. "Adam," he says with a nod.

"Jace," Adam replies, his tone slightly warning.

"I was just..." Jace trails off.

"You should apply," Adam repeats. "Don't you have a degree in literature? You could be helpful to the library. Are you planning to be around town more often?"

Jace shrugs. "My business is still predominantly in the city, but I could make monthly meetings. I'd love to help the library make more connections with some of the book-world folks in the city," Jace adds.

"Your marketing firm works with some publishers, yes?" Adam asks coolly.

"Yes, we do," Jace says.

"Seems like Jace here would make a good addition to your board," Adam says. I can see his jaw tic, but otherwise, he remains neutral, very un-Adam-like.

Jace looks from Adam to me and steps back. "I...I'll follow up with you next time I'm in town, Isa. Good to see you. And congrats again," Jace says, he gives an almost imperceptible nod to Adam and then walks away.

"Wow, driving and not pummeling Jace. Who are you?" I ask, my voice laced with a combination of surprise and admiration.

"A man who's been growing...a lot." He pauses and searches my eyes. Shit, why does he have to look so...hopeful?

"Isa, I wanted to take you over to the house. I mean, if you have a minute," he says, looking around us.

"I got it. Elisha just went to put the bakery stuff away. She said she'd help me break down our tent. Go," Ainsley urges, motioning with her hand for me to leave.

"You sure, kiddo? This tent is a pain in the ass."

She giggles. "I may have asked my brother and his friends to help."

I look over to see the group of boys who were cheering on Adam at the ice cream shop.

"Oh, look, it's Wellington! Dude, you're a freaking legend!" Ainsley's brother, Kaden, says.

I laugh. "Yeah, Mr. Wellington, a legend," I repeat, my voice mocking.

He groans. "Thanks, guys. Isa?" He puts out his arm and I tentatively take it, grabbing my bag as I wave to Ainsley. Ella is walking up with Elisha and she smiles at me. Elisha smirks and I give her a "what do you know that I don't" look. She shrugs and makes an angel halo over her head with her finger.

I roll my eyes. Adam opens the passenger car door and I climb inside.

When he gets in the driver's side, he looks over at me. "I swear to you, you were awarded that grant all on your own, Isa. But I did intentionally restore the house for you."

I nod and he drives us down the street and around the corner. It's honestly close enough to walk, but I decide to let him drive.

"So, you're driving again?" I ask.

"I am. I researched the safest vehicles and traded out all my cars for them. If I'm going to drive or have my loved ones in cars, then they will be indestructible."

"Adam...I mean, no car is..." I trail off as I glance at him.

"I know, but...watch," he says with a smirk. He stops the car and then reverses it on a side street straight into a construction barrel.

"Adam!" I screech as we hit it.

It's not hard, but I can't imagine it didn't make a small dent in his bumper.

He shrugs as he puts us back into drive and pulls us onto a short drive up to a gravel parking lot next to the house that

I've dreamed of buying for the library for five years. He parks and turns to me. "Come on," he says.

I'm still in shock that he just purposefully hit that barrel. I get out and see that he does have a small dent on his bumper. It's honestly not bad, so there must be something to say about this type of vehicle.

Adam presses a hand to it. "It's just metal and polymer," he says as he steps toward me. He cups my face. "I'm sorry, Isa. God, I'm sorry. I fucked up. I...just wanted to protect you, and instead, I pushed you away because I thought that was the only way I could protect you...to keep you away from me."

"But why?" I ask. "I..." I stop myself from confessing my love for him out of fear he won't feel the same way.

He visibly swallows and...is Adam Wellington nervous? No, I'm reading way too much into this.

"Follow me," he says as he steps back and holds out his hand. I tentatively take it. He leads me up the front path and opens the giant double doors. We step inside and my breath leaves my lungs. It's amazing, beautiful. I had seen construction equipment up here but I thought it was something to do with the commercial complex being built behind it. I never dreamed this was being turned into the perfect library space.

The main hall is set up for exhibits and an information desk and a checkout desk. He leads me through room after room. There's a children's section complete with a tree that the kids can climb up in and read in a secret reading nook. There are sections for thrillers and mysteries. Comfortable-looking chairs and ottomans are scattered about, inviting readers to sit and stay. I have actual meeting rooms for the community. There's Wi-Fi and state-of-the-art computers. It's...perfect.

"Follow me," he says as he squeezes my hand. I run my

fingers along the dark wood trim that makes me feel like I'm in an old building in Europe.

We step into a room on the far side of the house, and he pushes open a door and...

"Holy shit," I mutter as I look around us. It's a conservatory. There are roses, so many varieties of them. And a section with herbs, all with little signs about them. A few benches dot the room. It's quiet and peaceful and feels like I'm in a summer garden. And then I hear a rustling. I turn, and through the leaves of a small holly bush, I see them. Two cardinals.

I turn to Adam, confused.

"We found them in there. That tree had...grown on its own in here. We kept it and they stayed."

I smile. "Cardinals are...uh," I feel silly.

"Supposed to be our lost loved ones visiting us?" he asks, finishing my thought.

I nod. "Yep," I answer, letting the "p" pop.

"I know. Hell, maybe they are my parents saying they approve," he says with a lighthearted laugh.

I turn to him. "This is...it's more than I thought it could be," I say. "I...don't know what to say."

He steps up so we are nearly touching and takes my face in both of his big hands.

"Isa, you don't have to say a word." He pauses for a brief second and lets out a breath. "I love you, Isa. I don't know if it was the second you came barreling into my office or when your eyes lit up in my library or when I first kissed you, but I love you. I haven't stopped loving you. You saw the good in me, even when I didn't believe there was any good left. You saw past all my faults, and you let me be the real me. You accepted me just as I was, broken and all."

"You aren't broken, Adam," I whisper as I stare into his bright blue eyes.

"Maybe a little," he says with a smile, "but aren't we all?"

Shrugging, I nod.

"When I went to buy this property...I thought about this house, you'd mentioned it, but then it seemed too big a project and I didn't think it was possible. Then I realized, *I* was the only thing holding me back. That anything is possible, if you set your mind to it. You taught me that. You never gave up on those books you wanted. You never gave up on me. I shouldn't have pushed you away. And I don't know if you can forgive me for that, but...I'm going to try to make it up to you every day for the rest of my life if you give me another chance," he says.

"Adam?" I reply.

"Yes, beautiful?"

I blush as I smile. God, I've missed this man. "You are an irritating, alphahole. A rich jerk who has too much money for his own good. And you are way, way too controlling. But I think we can work on all those minor issues because...somehow, despite all of that, no matter how much you tried to make me dislike you, I fell in love with you. And even though I'm still mad at you, I'm still in love with you," I admit.

His grin widens. "You are?"

I give his chest a little shove. "I am, you big dummy. Are you always going to be this irritating?"

"Are you?" he asks, raising an eyebrow.

I giggle. "Yep."

"Well, then I guess we'll just have to be an irritating dummy and an irritating smarty-pants, together. Seems like a good duo to me," he says with a wink.

I smile up at him. "I suppose it does."

He leans down and I start to close my eyes anticipating his lips on mine.

"Isa?" he asks, his breath against my lips.

"What?" I ask, my voice laced with need.

"I am buying you a new car. Please for the love of God, let me win this argument. You can help pick it out, but please," he begs.

I laugh. "What if I say no?" I ask, keeping my eyes closed.

"Then a new one might just show up anyhow."

I shake my head. "You are impossible, Mr. Wellington."

His lips press to mine, and I can tell he's grinning. "But you wouldn't have it any other way, Ms. Garren," he says against my skin and then he kisses me. And I forget that I was mad at him, I forget about everything, except how much I love him, even when he is an irritating beast.

CHAPTER TWENTY-FIVE

Adam

Two months later...

"We're going to be late," I say from the stairwell.

"Give me two minutes!" Isa yells.

"That's Isa for forty-five minutes," Bastian says as he walks past me.

"If she's not down here in five minutes, I'm going up there and—"

"Ready," Isa says as she steps down toward me.

Bastian and I both look up at her. She looks beautiful, as always, but tonight she's glowing.

Bastian whistles and Isa giggles. I sweep her into my arms.

"You ready for this, beautiful?" I ask.

"Yes. So ready!" she says excitedly.

It's the official grand opening of the new library tonight. She's been working so hard, and I couldn't be prouder of her.

"Your father already messaged. They will meet us there in an hour," I say.

She rolls her eyes. "He's sent me about thirty texts today confirming the time. I think he's more nervous for me than I am."

"You have nothing to be nervous about. This is just a celebration. You've already done all the hard work," I point out.

"I know…I just…I can't believe this happened," she says. She looks up at me. "I owe it all to you."

I shake my head. "No, you owe it all to yourself. None of this would have happened if you hadn't hauled your ass over here in a snowstorm—"

"It wasn't storming when I left," she cuts me off as she rolls her eyes.

"Well, it all happened because you didn't give up on your dream," I state as I look into those warm brown eyes.

"I suppose," she says. She purses her lips as if contemplating it.

I lean my forehead against hers. "I know."

She grins and I press a quick kiss to her red-stained lips. "Come on, let's go celebrate your accomplishment."

She blushes but puts her arm through mine. "We'll meet you all over there," I say to Bastian and Mr. and Mrs. Potter as I open the front door and escort my girlfriend to our car. "You three behave," I add as we walk past Ames, Isaac, and Felipe who are all sitting by the front door in hopes they will get to go for a car ride.

Sliding into the driver's seat, I ponder just how far we've both come in just a few short months. While still completely humble, Isa has become a badass boss. She has four full-time employees now and still keeps four part-time employees and two volunteers. She just received her second grant and is working on an after-school reading program for children. She amazes me every day.

I drive us ten minutes to the library and park in Isa's reserved spot. It is still odd to have this be my normal. A loving girlfriend, me driving a car, and us opening a new library together. I couldn't have predicted this life if I had all the time in the world.

"You ready?" I ask.

"Yes. Let's do this," she says as she opens her car door. I hurry around to help her out, and then we head inside. Her staff are all there and we are quickly put to work helping with last-minute preparations.

Guests begin to arrive, and at exactly seven o'clock on the dot, Isa takes a microphone and stands on the landing of the giant staircase in the front foyer which has now become the information desk and checkout area.

"Good evening, Storyview Falls," she starts. A few people reply with "good evening" or nods.

"I can't tell you how very excited and pleased I am to be the first person to welcome you to the first new Storyview Falls Library in nearly one hundred years; ninety-seven to be exact." A few people laugh. "I'd be remiss if I didn't tell the story of how we got here. About three months ago, I was trying to talk a certain local man into sharing his very special book collection with us so that I might qualify for a match on a grant I desperately wanted to get for our library...well, to be fair, we desperately needed it. I was sure he wasn't going to oblige because I had sent ten emails with no more than a form response. So, one night, I picked up my dog from the groomer and I drove out to his estate and knocked on the door. And then I waited, and I waited some more, and eventually, my dog grew tired of waiting and took off toward this man's office." A few more people laugh. "And when I went running after him, I had no idea I would end up in Adam Wellington's office. I also had no idea that the snow flurries outside had turned into a full-on snowstorm that would strand me and my dog at this estate for nearly four days. And I'm still not completely sure how it happened, but somewhere between that first encounter and our winter book festival, I talked Mr. Wellington into giving me those books." She pauses and looks down at me. I smile up at her with pride. "Those books are now on permanent display in our exhibit hall, and I hope you all have a chance to view them tonight. Thanks to that grant, the donation of this new building, and a second grant, we are thriving, and we largely owe that to Mr. Adam Wellington. Let's give him a big round of applause," she urges as she claps her hands and everyone else joins in. I bow my head a little, but I keep my eyes on hers. She grins down at me. "I'm so thrilled to announce that just yesterday, I was able to confirm a new program for our little library. We will have a reading specialist joining our team next month and our goal is to provide an after-school reading program this coming fall." Everyone claps. "But tonight is really about celebrating how far we've come, so let's take time this evening to enjoy this amazing new space. Explore it, read, sit, and stay for a while...oh, and just for tonight we'll break some library rules and eat and dance, we have a band and a great caterer, thanks, Elisha, for providing the food for this evening. Enjoy your evening, and if you are able, we'd love to accept donations at our donation table. Thank you!"

Isa turns off the microphone and the band starts playing by a dance floor we cleared next to the largest of the meeting rooms to the right of the main hall.

"How was that?" she asks me as I take her in my arms.

"Perfect. You are perfect," I state, pulling her against me.

"Shall we dance?" she suggests. She pauses as we make our way across the room.

"Oh, one second, my parents made it," she says as she leads me over to them. We all say hello and small talk for a few minutes. Several other patrons pull Isa into conversations and an hour goes by before I manage to lead Isa to the dance floor.

"You are a popular librarian," I state as I begin to move us around the wooden floor.

She shrugs. "I suppose I am. Jealous?" she asks, raising her eyebrow.

"Nope," I reply and lean in to whisper in her ear. "Because they only get a few minutes of your time. And I'm going to get you all night, naked in my bed."

I watch as the pink creeps up her neck.

"Adam," she hisses.

"Yes?" I reply.

She looks up at me and smirks. "You are such a beast."

I lean down and press a quick kiss to her lips before pulling back to match her smirk. "And you wouldn't have it any other way."

EPILOGUE

Isa

Three months later...

"How big is your property? I feel like we've been riding Apollo and Cleo for three days," I ask.

Adam glances over at me. "Almost there," he states. "And for the record, it's only been thirty minutes. This trail is tricky."

"More like two hours and thirty minutes," I huff.

Adam clenches his jaw and I bite back a smile. It's become our norm. We push each other's buttons and I love every minute of it. I love that Adam doesn't back down and that he pushes me to be better. And I do the same for him. We're a team. I would have never imagined dating someone like him, yet now that he's a part of my life, I can't imagine living without him.

"There," Adam says. I follow the direction where he points, and I slow Cleo to a stop.

"It's…the falls?" I question as I slide off Cleo and walk to the edge of the water.

"Yes," he says as he joins me.

"Wait, you're telling me that this entire time, you knew where the real Storyview Falls were, and you never said anything?" I ask incredulously.

He shrugs and presses his lips together.

"Adam George Wellington!" I slap his arm and he laughs.

I stare back at the pond with a waterfall. There are lily pads and huckleberry bushes and wildflowers everywhere.

"It's so beautiful. You know the entire town thinks that dried-up waterfall over by the Peckering Cliffs is where the town got its name. But there's this rumor…" I trail off as I look back at the falls.

"That there were other falls that fed a magic pond?" I ask.

"Yeah, that contained the fountain of youth," I finish, my eyes widening. I turn to him. "Wait, this isn't a fountain of youth, is it?"

He laughs. "No. That part is *not* true."

"Bummer," I say as I look back at the pond. I see some cardinals on a tree, and I smile. "It's perfect here."

"There's just one thing that would make it more perfect," he says from behind me.

"What's that?" I ask. When I don't get an answer, I spin to look at him. My breath hitches as I find Adam on his knee, holding out the most beautiful garnet-and-diamond ring that I've ever seen.

"Isabelle Lisette Garren, you are the soul that completes mine. I didn't know how badly I needed you until I almost lost you just after finding you. I don't ever want to feel that loss again. I want to spend as much time as we have on this earth together, making it a better place. I want to play chess in the library and read in the conservatory and play with the dogs in the yard and eat Elisha's cookies and Leo's ice cream together. I just want to be with you, always. Please make me the happiest man on earth and be mine, be my wife?" he asks.

I look down into those brilliant blue eyes as mine fill with tears.

I nod. "Yes," I whisper.

"Yes?" he asks as if he misheard.

"Yes!" I cry out and jump into his arms knocking us to the ground.

He laughs and rolls us over. I hold up my hand and he slides the ring on it.

"I love it," I say as I admire it.

"It was my mother's," he says quietly.

"It's perfect," I reply as I grin at him.

"We're perfect," he adds as he leans down and kisses me. And just like that, I have my happily ever after.

Will Ella find her happily ever after? Find out in The Billionaire and the Maid.

And don't forget to grab your free copy of the Meet-Cute Mishap by joining my newsletter, plus receive freebies, give-aways, and so much more!

ABOUT THE AUTHOR

USA Today & International bestselling romance author, S.E. Rose lives near Washington D.C. with her family. When she's not wrangling her cats or keeping up with her kids, she's plotting her next story.

She loves all things wine, coffee, and cats. In her non-existent free time, she enjoys traveling, going to concerts, binging on her favorite shows, and reading, especially if it's a good mystery or comedy.

Learn more about upcoming books from S.E. Rose at www.seroseauthor.com.

Deceitful Destiny Series
Island (Book 1)
Secrets (Book 2)
Bravura (Book 3)
Determination (Book 4)
Home (Book 5)

The Poisoned Pawn World
A Fierce Princess
A Valiant Prince
A Wise Prince
A True King
The Overnight Naughty List

The Kingmakers of Kensington
A Man of Power
A Man of Wealth
A Man of Prestige

Perfectly Imperfect Love Series

Undeniably Perfect
Hopelessly Perfect
Romantically Perfect
Awkwardly Perfect
Reluctantly Perfect

Brides of Banneker
Scoring the One
Landing the One
Fixing the One

Once Upon a Billionaire Rom-Com Series
The Billionaire and the Librarian
The Billionaire and the Maid
The Billionaire and the Runaway

Fanning the Flames Series (Co-authored with Sierra Hill)
Burned (Book 1)
Ignited (Book 2)
Scorched (Book 3)

Clearview Falls University Series (Co-authored with Sierra Hill)
Falling for the Fake Boyfriend
Falling for the Roommate
Falling for the Football Player

Novels
Chronicles of a Hot Mess
Chronicles of a Rockin' Mess
The Decoy
Second Start (A Holiday Springs Resort Novel)

Novellas & Short Stories
    Neighbor in Apartment No. 5
    The Tinsel Tango
    The Fighter
    A Polar Pursuit (Vagabond Series)
    A Forward Holiday
    Misery Loves Company
    When It Rains, It Pours

Want to learn more? Visit www.seroseauthor.com.